Winter's Whispers

The Wicked Winters Book Ten

By
SCARLETT SCOTT

Winter's Whispers
The Wicked Winters Book 10

Edited by Grace Bradley
Cover Design by Wicked Smart Designs

For more information, contact author Scarlett Scott.
www.scarlettscottauthor.com

Don't miss this special addition to the bestselling *The Wicked Winters* series, featuring Winter family favorites and a whole lot of holiday steam!

Blade Winter is a coldhearted assassin with a deadly reputation. After a costly mistake leaves him banished to the countryside for a Christmas house party he has no wish to attend, he is furious. No amount of merrymaking is going to improve his mood. Until he crosses paths with a beautiful brunette he can never have, and suddenly, the prospect of a yuletide rusticating in Oxfordshire is not nearly as detestable...

Lady Felicity Hughes may be London's darling, but she is hiding a desperate secret. No one knows she must wed to save her family from penury, and she intends to keep it that way. But before she binds herself in a loveless marriage of convenience, she wants one night of passion. Who better to have it with than the wickedly handsome Mr. Winter?

Blade knows better than to dally with a lady who is forbidden, no matter how much she tempts him. Felicity is equally determined to get what she wants, even if there can be no future between herself and a dangerous man like Blade. She has nothing left to lose. Except her heart.

Dedication

For Anna & Sadie

Chapter One

Oxfordshire, 1814

THERE WAS A female under his bed.

Trouble, warned his instincts.

A female was what had landed Blade here, in the monkery, at a cursed country house party being held by his half brother Devereaux Winter.

Not this particular one, though. He would have recognized the ankles. Blade was a connoisseur of ankles. And knives. Not necessarily in that order.

This one's ankles were fine-boned, nicely turned, covered in pale stockings. He noted those first. He noted her arse second. A plummy handful, that. Too bad it was draped in an unappealing gown of virginal white. Virgins weren't his sort.

Innocence wasn't his sort.

Blade preferred debauched. Sinful widows, wicked wives. A woman who wasn't afraid to suck a cock.

Which was why the miss rooting about beneath his bed needed to go. At once.

He cleared his throat, hoping the strange bit of petticoats would realize she was no longer alone. But she did not emerge. Instead, she wriggled about, emphasizing the tempting qualities of her ankles and rump. *Damn.* Too bloody bad he was here to stay out of trouble. Those ankles presented a strong temptation to create an exception to his rule.

There was a muffled sound emerging from the bed now. He closed the door at his back and strode nearer, drawn by a combination of perplexity and attraction. *By God*, was the woman having a conversation? Under his bed?

"Miss Wilhelmina, do come," the strange creature was saying in a sweet, cajoling voice that would have certainly worked wonders upon Blade. She had the voice of an angel, this one. "I shall give you liver, I promise."

The devil?

Blade crouched down by the shapely bottom, curiosity triumphing over patience. "What the hell is under my bed?"

"Ahhhh!"

Her scream was muffled, but the jolt that went through her body was evident, as was the undeniable sound of her head connecting with the wooden slats on the underside of the bed.

She muttered something that sounded suspiciously like an epithet.

If he were a gentleman, he would cease ogling her arse, but he wasn't, so he kept watching as she wiggled, slowly emerging. He had never been much concerned about a woman's derriere, but there was something about this one that was mesmerizing. He imagined cupping it in his hands, shaping and molding it.

Not now, Blade, you bloody sot. It is not the time to get a cockstand when there is an innocent miss hiding beneath the bed along with a creature she has promised liver.

As she sidled her way from under the bed, he could not help also admiring the manner in which her gown and petticoats were bunching up as she went, revealing more and more of her curved, stocking-clad legs. She was deliciously shapely, but that was not something he ought to be noticing either.

The duel he had fought with the Earl of Penhurst had

been enough for his half brother Dom to banish him from London and their gaming hell, The Devil's Spawn. Petticoats were dangerous, and he did not need any more problems than those which currently bogged him down.

Still, it did not help when the creamy skin of her thighs, just above her stockings, was exposed. Nor did it do a whit of good when she finally emerged, a dark-haired beauty with wide, hazel eyes and the most inviting pair of pink lips he had ever seen. To say nothing of her bosom, spilling over the top of her modest gown. Apparently, her foray beneath his bed had also rendered her bodice askew. Her cheeks were prettily flushed. Everything about the woman who had slithered from beneath his bed was delectable.

This was going to be a problem. He could bloody well sense it.

"Sir!" She rubbed her head. "It was terribly rude of you, speaking without announcing your presence. I may have done myself great injury."

Incredible.

The baggage was taking him to task. She was a lady, that much he could spy instantly. Her gown was fine, though not as bang up to the mark as Lady Penhurst's fashion. Her voice was cool, clipped.

Aristocratic.

He passed his hand along his jaw, allowing his gaze to roam over her freely. "Reckon the rude one is the one who stuffed herself under my bed."

Her flush deepened, creeping down her throat. "I am attempting to rescue Miss Wilhelmina."

"Miss Wilhelmina," he repeated.

Mayhap her wits were addled. He had yet to see a sign of anything under the bed save her.

"My kitten." She struggled with her gown, belatedly

covering her limbs.

A feline. He was appalled. Cats were detestable animals. The offer of liver finally made sense.

"Christ." His lip curled. "Get it out of here."

She frowned at him. "That is what I was trying to do when you interrupted me, sir."

"Blade," he corrected, sketching a mocking bow. "No sir. No mister."

Her frown deepened, that hazel gaze of hers—not quite green, nor brown, yet almost gray—searched his. "I beg your pardon?"

"The name's Blade Winter. Half brother to the host. Reluctant guest. Ardent hater of cats," he listed off each fact idly, watching, fascinated by her in spite of himself. "Definitely not the sort of cove you ought to find yourself alone with, in a bedchamber."

Her brows rose. The becoming pink flush had reached the tops of her breasts now. "Oh dear."

Bloody hell. Mayhap a fortnight trapped in the wintry wilds of England was not going to be nearly as boring as he had supposed.

What a sophisticated, genteel miss thing to say, *oh dear.* As if they were in the drawing room and she had struck a discordant note on the pianoforte or whatever the hell it was that fancy nibs and ladies did together. Blade wouldn't know. All he did with fancy ladies who dressed in silk and smelled of sweet perfume was bed them.

"Fetch the liver," he told her, irritated that she remained, tempting, wide-eyed, and within reach.

Nettled that desire was sliding through him, even now, when he could plainly see she was the last sort of lady with whom he would ever dally.

"Liver?" She blinked.

"Eavesdropping is a talent of mine, especially when there's a lady stuffed beneath my bed, having a chat with her cat while her arse hangs in the wind," he said scathingly, just to see if her flush would deepen.

She gasped. "How dare you? My *bottom* was most certainly not *hanging in the wind.*"

He could not contain his grin at her prim refusal to say the word arse, which just made him want to remark upon it more. "No need to worry, sweetheart. It's a plummy arse you've got."

"Plummy!" Her color heightened. Her lips parted.

"Careful. Wouldn't want to catch flies, eh?" He cocked his head, considering her, his gaze dipping to her bosom once more. And a fine bosom it was, indeed. That the front and upper half of her was every bit as good as the lower back was both a source of appreciation and irritation.

Appreciation because he was Blade Winter, and he excelled at two skills: fighting and fucking. Irritation because the latter of those two skills was one in which he could not currently afford to indulge.

Stupid bloody duel.

He was an expert marksman—came with the trade—and if that twat Penhurst hadn't moved, his bullet would have grazed his left arm as planned, only enough to put a rip in the coat sleeve rather than enough to make him bleed. And potentially lose the limb.

"Would you go, please?" the interloper in his chamber asked in her perfect, aristocratic English.

Surely he had misheard her.

"Pardon?"

"Miss Wilhelmina will be too fearful to emerge with a stranger here."

He still could not believe she had named a cat Miss

bloody Wilhelmina. It was something only a pampered lady would do, one who had never needed to worry where her next meal would come from. One who had never feared the shadows in the night. One who had never suffered a moment in her privileged life.

"Too fucking bad for Miss Wilhelmina," he snapped, in a foul mood at the reminder of his cursed past. "This is my chamber, and she is not welcome here. Nor are you. I don't tup virgins, and even if I did, you aren't my sort, sweetheart."

He was being rude, he knew. He had cursed and referenced all manner of things not fit for a proper lady's ears. But Blade Winter wasn't a gentleman. And he was only rusticating in the midst of nothing in Oxfordshire because Dom had strong-armed him into it.

As the leader of the bastard Winters, the eldest of them all, and the one who ran The Devil's Spawn, Dom made such decisions. The rest of them fell in line like good little soldiers. Even if it meant being sent to the monkery where strange, lovely ladies were rummaging about beneath their beds in search of cats with preposterous names.

"There is no cause to use such language, sir, or to be so ungenerous," the lady in question said now, her tone frosty enough to rival the wintry winds buffeting the outside of this massive old cavern of a home.

"I've been traveling for two days, and this is the last place I want to be," he pointed out, punctuating his words with an annoyed sigh. "Enough talking, madam. I will extract the beast myself."

He noted the carpet was thick and new. Fine, too. Of course it was. Nothing but the best for old Dev. Blade tried to temper the bitterness festering inside him whenever he thought of the legitimate heir to the Winter fortune.

Devereaux Winter had been born on the right side of the

blanket, the eldest and only legitimate son of their father, a merciless merchant who owned half of London by the time he had cocked up his toes. But neither the bastard Winters—Dom, Devil, Blade, Demon, Genevieve, and Gavin—nor the legitimate Winters—Devereaux, Pru, Eugie, Grace, Bea, and Christabella—had been aware of one another until their sainted sire's death.

"You cannot fetch Miss Wilhelmina," the vexing woman intruding upon his solace said, cutting through Blade's thoughts.

"Well, you are not fetching her, are you?" he pointed out. "And I want my chamber back. Stands to reason one of us has to get the damned thing, and it may as well be me."

She bit her lower lip, drawing his attention to the ripe succulence of her mouth. She had the sort of lips made for kissing, no denying it. And though she wasn't his sort—he hadn't been lying about that—he found himself drawn to her in a most unwanted way. A most dangerous way, too.

She is not for you, Blade. Virgins make your cock shrivel.

Most of them did. Pity this one didn't. Then again, mayhap she was no virgin at all, but a bored wife. The prospect improved his mood. She appeared young, and the pale-ivory gown suggested an innocent, but he had reached an assumption about her too soon.

"She will claw you, Mr. Winter," she warned. "I found her, lost and wandering, and she is quite suspicious of anyone aside from myself. Please, it is best if I fetch her."

"Reluctant to be returned to your loving arms, is she?" He quirked a brow, trying to ignore how radiant she was at this proximity, how her sweet scent of jasmine invaded his senses. "I am afraid I do not know your name, and if I am to rescue your feline, I ought to have that, at least. Do you not think?"

Her nostrils flared, and he was struck by the most ridiculous urge to kiss the tip of her nose. He banished the unworthy thought. As nonsensical as the name of her cat.

"Lady Felicity Hughes," she said, giving him a name at last.

Hughes.

Blade knew the name. The bastard Winters were in the business of earning as much coin as they could from the quality, and it behooved them to stay informed. Her papa was the Earl of Harding. Pockets to let. Bad gambling habit, that old cur. Had three daughters, all in desperate need of husbands. The eldest was a diamond of the first water.

Lady Felicity.

Blade had never crossed paths with her, limited as he was to Cyprian balls and wicked house parties for the depraved. Until now.

She *was* a virgin, damn it.

There went all his fun.

His lip curled. "I'll be fetching Miss Wigglesby now, my lady."

He lowered himself, belly first to the carpet—dreadfully annoying position when his cock was hard—and slid beneath the bed.

"MISS WILHELMINA," FELICITY corrected the outrageous bounder whose room she was unintentionally intruding upon.

But her words did not seem to reach him, for the tall, lean man was already slipping beneath the bed. She could not wrest her gaze from him, no matter how inappropriate it was for her to be alone with this uncouth man. His breeches were fitted to his long legs perfectly, showing off his muscular thighs and calves. To say nothing of his bottom.

That reminded her.

He had remarked upon her bottom. Had claimed it had been in the wind. The man was a devil. An ill-mannered, ill-tempered boor.

Also handsome.

Desperately, rakishly so. A golden-haired Adonis, with a surly disposition. That was her ill fortune, little Miss Wilhelmina—who was not supposed to be present at this house party to begin with—hiding herself beneath this man's bed.

Felicity shuddered.

And that was when she realized her bosom had almost fallen out of her décolletage. She had been putting on a shocking display. That devil! His eyes had been wandering all over her as he said nary a word.

She tugged at her bodice, frantically hauling it upward. That was the problem with having a generous bosom. She was forever attempting to hide it. Truly, she ought to have donned a fichu before she had gone traipsing after Miss Wilhelmina. But she had been too distressed to think of anything else when she had noticed the kitten missing.

"There you are," Mr. Winter growled from beneath the bed. "I've got you now."

More shifting—Felicity averted her gaze, which wanted to linger on his distressingly masculine form, then stole one last glance at the way his breeches clung lovingly to his backside—and he had emerged, holding Miss Wilhelmina aloft by the scruff of her neck.

Felicity took the poor darling from him at once, cuddling her precious ball of fur to her bosom. When in need of a fichu, the kitten would do. Soft, gray fur, purring like mad, warm and beloved, nestled against her. "That is no way to hold a kitten, Mr. Winter," she chastised, aware of his eyes on her.

She was overheated.

Why was it so dreadfully hot in here?

Why could she not stop being fascinated by the fullness of his lips?

"That is how the mother cat moves them about," said those lips. "Now do run along, Lady Francine. I do not like cats or trespassers."

She frowned. How lowering. The mannerless rogue had already forgotten her name. "Lady Felicity, sir. And how can you dislike cats? Do you not have a soul?"

"I expect not."

His response should have been a warning she ought not to linger, now that she had Miss Wilhelmina back where she belonged. But as the eldest of three sisters who had been motherless from the time Esme had been born, Felicity had been doing what she should for far too long.

This country house party was her last chance to experience the smallest modicum of freedom before she would have to wed.

"Surely there must be good in you somewhere, Mr. Winter," she allowed. "You just rescued Miss Wilhelmina."

"Selfish," he clipped. "I want you and the feline gone."

Despicably rude would have been more apt. His curt words stung.

"We shall not burden you a moment more, then." With as much elegance as she could summon—as it turned out, not much when she was flustered and clutching a cat to her bosom—she rose to her feet.

He remained where he was, idly sprawled on the floor without showing a hint of deference to the fact that she was a lady. Just who was this Mr. Winter? A scoundrel and a rogue, it was certain. He rested his forearm on his knee as if he had not a care in the world, tilting his head, his strikingly blue-gray eyes perusing her once more.

Forcing herself to dip into a curtsy, she tipped up her chin. "Good day, Mr. Winter. Thank you for finding Miss Wilhelmina."

He raised a brow. "Keep the creature where it belongs, Lady Francesca."

Dreadful man. Was he getting her name wrong intentionally? She would not doubt it.

This time, she swept from the chamber without bothering to correct him.

Chapter Two

*T*HE LAST PERSON Blade wanted to see was Devereaux Winter.

Then again, mayhap the luscious, cat-smuggling Lady Felicity was the last person Blade wanted to see. Small creatures, particularly innocent ones who looked up at him with trusting, hazel eyes, made him want to punch something. And that went for both the lady and the ridiculously named kitten. Their gazes were irritatingly similar.

"I trust you are not going to cause any trouble for either my family or my guests," Winter was saying now in warning tones.

"Thought it was my family, too," he could not resist pointing out, before taking a sip of his drink only to realize it was negus.

Blade spit the offensive stuff back into his cup. Where was some sturdy gin or smuggled Scots whisky when one needed it?

Winter looked distinctly unimpressed. "You do not care for negus?"

"No man with ballocks does," Blade informed his half brother, not giving a damn that he was being rude.

He did not bloody well want to be here, and he did not bloody well like Devereaux Winter. His half sisters were tolerable. The red-haired one, Christabella, was a duchess with a propensity for saying ridiculous things. He liked her well enough. The rest… Well, Blade was still deciding what he thought of them.

Each sister was married to a lord, with the exception of the youngest, Bea, who was married to Winter's business partner. Merrick Hart was a fine enough fellow; Blade reckoned all the lords had fire pokers up their arses. One of them, the Earl of Something—Blade couldn't recall the name and the man hadn't stepped foot inside their establishments, so he may as well not exist—was frowning at him now as if Blade had just produced an East End rat from his pocket.

"I can assure you that I have ballocks, and can nonetheless enjoy the stuff," Winter was saying.

"Married life making you soft," Blade muttered, setting the cup down upon a nearby table. "Haven't you whisky?"

"Of course I have whisky."

Thank Christ. How the hell would he have lasted for a fortnight in the monkery without getting proper spoony drunk?

"I'll have some of that instead, if you please, brother." He cast an insincere smile in Devereaux Winter's direction, knowing it would nettle.

Not caring.

"Before you have a drop, you will promise me you shall not cause so much as a crumb of a crumb's worth of trouble," Winter countered.

"Hmm." Blade pretended to ponder those words. "What about a crumb of a *crumb* of a crumb?"

"No trouble," Winter growled.

"Pardon me, but you do not look like the sort of gentleman who is adept at keeping himself from any sort of trouble at all," said Earl of Something.

Adept. Fancy cove's word. Blade thought he knew what it

meant.

"I ain't a gentleman," he said unapologetically, plucking his favorite knife from within his coat and lightly stroking his thumb over the blade.

It was a gesture not intended to intimidate. Rather, Blade's knives calmed him. It was an old habit, born from his days on the street before Devil and Dom found him. Best to walk about the rookeries with one's hand on a weapon, especially for lads who had been built like a bean as he had once been. Those lads were easily overpowered. Fortunately, time and effort had strengthened him. He no longer required the knives unless he had a job to carry out. And even then, a pistol was a far preferable weapon.

Not that he expected to have need of any sorts of weapons at this tedious affair.

He was trapped here. Nowhere to escape to. Nothing but snow, aristocrats, family members he was only beginning to tolerate, and a virgin with a goddamn cat.

He suppressed a shudder.

"You shall be a gentleman for the duration of the house party," Winter told him. "That was understood, along with all your invitations."

"You invited us because your wife wanted it, and she keeps your ballocks in her reticule," Blade taunted.

Everyone knew Devereaux Winter was hopelessly besotted with his wife. If Lady Emilia asked him to jump into the Thames in the heart of winter, the poor sot would take a dive. And likely drown, more fool he.

Winter's nostrils flared. "You will speak respectfully. Lady Emilia is my wife, and she has the heart of an angel."

"Would have to, if she is married to the likes of you," Blade said.

But instead of being outraged, Winter grinned. "Cannot

argue. I am damned fortunate she is my wife."

May the Lord preserve him from ever becoming so stupid about a set of petticoats.

Inexplicably, Blade's mind traveled to thoughts of the deliciously lovely Lady Felicity. Of her legs, her wriggling rump. Her bosom. Those lips. Her flashing hazel eyes.

He should have kissed her yesterday when he had the opportunity.

Bloody hell, what was he thinking? He most certainly should not have kissed her. Not because he gave a damn about Devereaux Winter's edicts, but because he did care about remaining in good standing with Dom and Devil and the rest of his siblings. They had all been infuriated by the results of his ill-advised duel. Consigning himself to hell—er, Oxfordshire—was his way of making amends.

"I know the feeling all too well," the Earl of Something said to Winter.

The taste of negus was sickeningly sweet on Blade's tongue. The ridiculous way the two other men in the room cared for their wives was equally repulsive.

"I promise to behave," he snapped. "Now where the devil is the whisky?"

At least Demon, Gavin, and Genevieve would be arriving soon. Dom and his wife had just had a babe, and Devil and Lady Evie were expecting their first child any day, which had precluded them from traveling to the countryside. Blade had been sent early, thanks to that damned duel.

"I am afraid a promise is not sufficient," Winter said, cocking his head. "I think we need to be certain he shan't cause any problems for the next fortnight, don't you, Hertford?"

Ah, *Hertford*.

The Earl of Something was the bloody Earl of Hertford.

The earl nodded. "How do you suppose we can make certain he will be the perfect gentleman?"

Blade's throat was getting itchy. His cravat was too damned tight. Tied by a servant Winter had sent to him that morning. Called himself a valet. Blade had never heard of the like.

"Excellent question," Winter said to the earl, as if they were conducting a dialogue without Blade's presence. "Mayhap we should take his knife."

Fuck. Blade's thumb stilled on the knife. This was his favorite blade. His lucky blade. It never left his side. He slipped it into his coat. "Not unless you fancy a broken wrist during your house party, *milord.*"

Winter's jaw tightened, the only sign Blade's insult had hit its mark. Deveraux Winter was not an aristocrat; he'd never be a lord. This sprawling estate and manor house had belonged to his wife's father, the duke, before he had purchased it. But one could not buy a title.

"Something else," Hertford suggested briskly, as if one of the most dangerous men in London had not just threatened the both of them.

He was *adept* at blending into the scenery. It was what Blade did, how he reached his targets. Namely, Winter enemies. And there it was, he had used a fancy cove's word in his own thoughts.

Damn it.

"My word. That ought to be enough," he gritted. "We are family, are we not?"

Including the earl. Which was quite bloody rich. The laugh of the century, at least.

"No dallying with the guests," his half brother ordered.

Devereaux Winter could have passed for Dom's twin. They were both tall, broad, fierce. Dark-haired, dark-eyed, and commanding. Both the leaders of their respective Winter clans. And they had the same thoughts, the same rigid adherence to their wives and honor.

"Surely there may be some married ladies in attendance who require…distraction," Blade tried.

"No," Winter bellowed.

"You are fortunate you did not kill Penhurst in that foolish duel," the earl added.

Hell. The Earl of Hertford was a prude. And Devereaux Winter a killjoy.

"I am an unrivaled marksman," he said. "The idiot moved."

"Nevertheless, you can agree you have caused enough difficulties for our family," Winter said.

"Now it is *our* family," Blade grumbled, plainly seeing the difference. "What do you want from me? Shall I carve a promise into my flesh? I came here to calm the waters, not to bedevil them. All I want is whisky and a comfortable place to avoid everyone for the next thirteen days."

Hertford and Winter exchanged a look.

Blade read it. Disbelief.

Fair enough; his reputation *was* black.

"I promise," he bit out. "You have my word. If I cause any trouble for you, I will give you all my weapons and my head on a pike. Trust me, I have had more than my fair share of trouble and quim both these last few weeks. All I seek is forgiveness."

Once more, Lady Felicity's face rose in his mind. Haunting, tempting, taunting.

He thrust all thoughts of her away and held his half brother's gaze.

Devereaux Winter studied him for a long time. At last, he nodded. "I trust you, Blade. Do not disappoint me."

Well, hell. Mayhap wealthy nibs like his half brother did not understand that sooner or later, everyone in one's life was a source of disappointment. But never mind that. He would learn the lesson in his own time, and hopefully Blade would not be the one to do the teaching.

All he had to do was keep to himself.

That ought to be easy.

FELICITY ROUNDED A corner in the hall and ran into something tall, hard, warm, and smelling of leather and…citrus and musk.

Mr. Blade Winter.

She would recognize that maddening scent anywhere.

Her palms instinctively flattened against the muscled wall of his chest. She ought to retract them, but there was something about the dratted man that lured her just as it had the day before. His heat seared her.

She pressed herself nearer. For one reckless moment only. Her breasts collided with him, their hips connecting. The air fled her lungs.

Hands gripped her waist, steadying her. His impossibly blue gaze settled on hers.

"Lady Frances," came that deep, wondrous baritone.

Mocking.

Had he truly forgotten her name once more, or was he merely toying with her? She stared up into his handsome, unreadable countenance, and could not determine which it was.

"Lady Felicity," she corrected, mustering all the chill she possessed.

But inside, *oh,* inside, she was aflame.

From a touch, from a collision, from a man she otherwise found arrogant and ill-mannered. An insolent lout. It made no sense. What drew her to him? And why was she not retreating, stepping away, removing her palms from his chest? Why was she instead coasting them over the broad plane, absorbing his warmth and strength?

"Lady Felicity," he repeated, his tone intimate. His gaze settled on her lips, and it felt like a caress. Or a kiss.

She was breathless. Mindless. An imbecile. My goodness, had she been *caressing* his chest? Felicity yanked her hands away, then gathered her wits and took a step in retreat.

A step in haste, it would appear. She had forgotten she had been carrying a stack of books when she had rounded the corner, and they had fallen to the floor during the course of her impact with Mr. Winter. Now, she tripped over one of them.

It was too late to compensate. She lost her balance and went down on her back in a rustle of silk.

Acute embarrassment washed over her. She had landed upon her rump with unforgiving force, and pain radiated out, cementing her humiliation. She was not ordinarily so graceless. Indeed, all she had to recommend herself was her face and her elegance, since there was no dowry to speak of. How was she going to land a husband at this cursed house party—as she must do, for time was running out—if she could not keep from making a cake of herself before this rogue?

She expected his laughter. More mockery.

But instead, he thrust a hand out.

She eyed it. There was a strange marking peeking from beneath his sleeve, atop his hand. On his skin... Why, it looked like a dagger, drawn on his flesh. She stared, fascinated. Heat slid through her with the torpor and sweetness of honey.

His hand was large, callused. His fingers long. For a wild moment, she wondered what that hand would feel like upon her.

"Do you intend to sit on the floor all day?" he asked, the rough baritone of his voice startling her from her foolish reverie.

Of course, even in his offer of gentlemanly aid, he found a way to be surly.

She settled her hand in his, the contact sending a strange sense of awareness through her. A frisson, sweeping up her arm, then down her spine, before ultimately pooling between her thighs. He pulled her to her feet in one easy motion, so quickly she felt dizzied for a brief, disconcerting moment.

Or mayhap that was just the effect he had upon her.

"Thank you, Mr. Winter," she found the wits to say.

He grinned, and the heat between her thighs flared once more. *Good heavens*, the rascal was truly beautiful in a wicked, tempting way she had never seen in another gentleman.

She had to get ahold of herself. Calm her rapidly beating heart. She had come here to find a husband, and one with funds enough to support her younger sisters in their debuts, to offer them a dowry so they could make proper matches. Not to flirt with unacceptable strangers.

"Going to give me my hand, or do you intend to keep it?" he queried wryly.

Her cheeks were on fire. She dropped his hand as if it were fashioned of flame too. It may as well have been. This man would burn her. Ruin her. She knew it then and there.

"Forgive me," she mumbled, then busied herself with the business of collecting the books she had dropped in their impact.

Stupid Felicity. Two years on the marriage mart, and hailed a beauty, a fine marital prize. And yet, she had squandered every chance for a husband because she had so foolishly believed she had time. That Papa's debts were not as monumental as they were. She had been waiting for love. Now she would have to settle for a comfortable income. And there was no surer way to lose this last, precious chance than to dally with uncouth rogues.

She had to think of Esme and Cassandra.

But Mr. Winter did not leave her to her misery. Instead, he sank to his haunches and helped her retrieve the books. Even his presence burned through her, along with his scent. He was so maddeningly attractive. It was not his face, but something indefinable about him. He possessed an air of mystery, charm, and mayhem that was unspeakably compelling.

For all the wrong reasons.

He handed the books to her, and she rose to her feet. "Thank you, sir."

He stood with her, lingering. Not bowing and moving on. Just staring at her in that way he had. Assessing and yet…intimate. His stare was like a touch.

She ought to flee. To curtsy and go. They were in one of the massive halls of Abingdon House, alone, and anyone could come upon them. It would be quite disastrous, if innocent enough.

And yet, she stayed. Drawn to him. Icarus, flying too near the sun.

"Is there something else you wished to say, Mr. Winter?" she asked, cursing herself for the breathlessness in her voice.

His lips twitched. "Where is Miss Whistlewhiskers?"

His impertinent question wrung a laugh from her. "Whistlewhiskers?"

"Aye." His grin deepened. "What was I thinking? That would be a spoony name for a cat, wouldn't it, my lady?"

"Spoony?" She frowned at him, telling herself the dimple in his right cheek was not nearly as alluring as the warmth in her belly suggested it was.

"Crazy," he elaborated.

"Are you suggesting Miss Wilhelmina is a crazy name for a kitten, sir?"

The dimple remained, taunting her. "I'd never."

Drat the man, his rough accent—decidedly not aristocratic, hinting at his antecedents—was somehow intriguing. His voice was mellow and deep, pleasing to her ears. Even when he was being rude.

He was not being terribly rude at the moment, however, and it only served to heighten her confusion. And her attraction. When he chose to charm, good heavens…

"I think you are teasing me, Mr. Winter," she said, clutching her books to her chest.

Auntie Agatha was probably looking for her. She was Felicity's chaperone for this country house party. Rather remiss at her task, it was true. But eventually, she noted Felicity's absence. She would likely be noting it by now.

Felicity really ought to go at once, instead of remaining here in this maddening man's presence.

He leaned nearer, stealing her breath once more. "If I were teasing you," he said slowly, lowering his head so that he was devastatingly close, "you would know it, Lady Felicity."

He had gotten her name right that time.

But that wasn't what was making her dizzy. Or what was making her sway toward him, until his breath coasted over her lips in the prelude to a kiss she wanted, no matter how much she shouldn't.

It was the connection between them. She had felt it yesterday, in his chamber. A stunning sense of awareness, a remarkable difference, when their gazes had first clashed. She had told herself it was impossible. She had blamed her response on the blow she had taken to the head when she had rapped it beneath his bed.

She realized she had been wrong. Because it was still here, simmering between them. Growing bigger and more pronounced with each passing second.

"You are terribly forward, sir," she murmured, as if it were an insult.

It was not.

She wanted him to be more forward.

To kiss her.

No, Felicity. You must not. Remember why you have come here, Esme and Cassandra. You need a husband. This beautiful scoundrel is not what you need.

"I pride myself on it," the devil said with a smirk.

A smirk that told her he knew the effect he had upon her.

She blinked, forcing herself from whatever spell had settled over her. She could not afford to make a mistake. To be ruined. Felicity clutched the books to her chest as if they were a shield.

"I have no doubt you do," she managed, dipping into a passable curtsy.

If Auntie Agatha had witnessed it, she would have scolded her. The form was all wrong. Then again, if Auntie Agatha had witnessed any of Felicity's behavior just now, she would have likely packed them into the first carriage headed back for London.

Reminding herself of her duty, Felicity skirted Mr. Winter and continued on her way to the library, feeling his too-blue gaze on her with every step she took.

Chapter Three

"*I* DID TELL you not to bring that cat, did I not, my dear girl?" Auntie Agatha asked, pinning Felicity with an imperious frown.

Sigh.

Felicity hugged Miss Wilhelmina to her and faced her august aunt. Auntie Agatha had insisted upon inspecting her morning toilette before she headed to the breakfast table. She was father's older sister, widowed, white-haired, and given to prodigious churlishness. Mayhap the cause of that was the arthritis that often kept her bound to her chair, if not relying heavily upon her cane.

"But she is my companion," Felicity argued.

"She has escaped thrice," her aunt countered, disapproval dripping from her voice. "And how shall you snare yourself a husband when you are covered in cat fur?"

Felicity glanced down at her bodice, which did indeed have a few strands of gray fur stuck to it. "I shall change before breakfast."

"It is best you should." Auntie Agatha cast a dismissive glance over her. "This gown makes your bosom look far too large and your hips too wide."

But her bosom *was* large, and her hips *were* wide.

Felicity bit her tongue, quelling the urge to offer a retort. Miss Wilhelmina offered a purr of commiseration.

"At least you do not have your mother's face. Rounder than a saucer of tea is not an attractive shape. Esme and Cassandra, however…they shall need more help, I fear. The finest dresses to distract from the rest of them." Auntie Agatha raised a brow, making an expansive gesture that was somehow elegant and rude all at once. "Why do you not wear more ivory, my dear? Daffodil makes everyone look sallow, yourself included."

"Yellow is a cheerful color," Felicity dared to argue, for it put her in mind of happier days and summer sun, flowers blooming in spring.

The promise of renewal.

Hope, which was becoming increasingly fleeting for Felicity with each day that passed.

"A color cannot be cheerful, dearest," Auntie Agatha dismissed. "Besides, cheer is a dreadful state, best reserved for the simple-minded and babes. The rest of us know what we are in for. Wear the jaconet muslin trimmed with Vandyke lace, if you please. It is most becoming."

A rare compliment from Auntie Agatha.

"And a lady who is desperate must be as fetching as possible," her aunt added.

As usual, the compliment was wrapped in an insult. Felicity ought to have known.

"Am I not fetching enough?" she asked. "I had no end of suitors in London."

"Two seasons, and you turned them all away. Even a diamond of the first water must choose from her beaux, lest they start defecting. Do you think the farmer wishes to chase about the cow for two years before he can milk it?" Auntie Agatha asked, her tone queenly.

"Forgive me for thinking myself the better of a milk cow," she said.

25

"Never mind the analogy, dearest." Auntie Agatha thumped her cane on the floor. "*Reward.* That is the promise you have to dangle before all gentlemen. Marriage to you is a great reward, and you must show them it is such. If you wait too long, you shall end up a spinster, and goodness knows what shall become of your sisters. It is your duty to them, to your father, to yourself, to make a good match."

A good match.

Felicity sighed aloud this time rather than only in her mind. She was reluctant to ask what Auntie Agatha's notion of a good match would be. For some reason, Blade Winter rose in her mind. Auntie Agatha would be properly horrified to discover she had consorted with such a man. As it was, she had been scarcely able to conceal her disgust over the *common stock*, as she had phrased it, of some of the guests in attendance.

You will not know them, she had added for good measure. *Speak only to the gentlemen in attendance.*

By which she had meant the lords, of course.

But that was the trouble. Felicity *wanted* to know the common stock. Or rather, one of them in particular.

"Lord Foy is in attendance," Auntie Agatha went on. "And there is Lord Denton as well. Excellent prospects, the both of them, despite the latter having been jilted by the Duke of Linross's daughter. Flighty chits, the both of them."

Felicity scratched Miss Wilhelmina's soft head, her aunt's recommendations droning on.

HIS HALF SISTER, Lady Aylesford, held the infant toward him as if conveying to him the world's greatest prize. If there was one creature Blade disliked more than cats, it was babies.

He stared at the chubby cheeks, the soft skin, the white cap and swaddling. "No."

"Go on," she said. "Lady Gwendolyn shan't bite. You are her uncle, you know."

Christ, he supposed he was. As he stared at the miniature person still being offered, something unexpected slid through him.

Emotion?

Tenderness?

"Uncle," he said stupidly.

The child looked delicate. He was a rough man. His hands were only accustomed to gentleness when skimming the lush curves of a woman's body. Did not Lady Aylesford realize he could drop the thing?

"Yes, Uncle Blade," said his spoony half sister, smiling at him. "Hold her, if you please. Though you must tell me your real Christian name. No one is called Blade."

"I am." He made no move to accept the child, but he had to admit Lady Gwendolyn was rather…sweet-looking. She cooed and made a sound of contentment, then stuffed her fist into her little mouth and sucked on it.

"I refuse to believe it," Lady Aylesford continued if he had not spoken. "Do hold out your arms, you silly man. Settle yourself on the settee like so. Excellent."

Blade found himself seated on the furniture in question, arms positioned to welcome the babe. Suddenly, his niece— half niece—was a soft, warm weight in his arms.

It was…astonishing.

Her blue eyes blinked up at him, and she grinned.

"Uncle Blade shall do fine."

"Oh, she is in love with you already," Lady Aylesford said, smiling. "You need not have fretted so about holding her. William?"

He realized she was attempting to guess his Christian name. "Blade."

"Peter?"

"Blade."

Her nose wrinkled. "John?"

He sighed. Little Lady Gwendolyn grabbed his coat in her fist and tugged. "*Blade*, Lady Aylesford."

"Oh, do cease being formal with me," she said, with a dismissive wave of her hand. "You must call me Grace."

The woman was stubborn; he admired that. When Genevieve arrived, he had no doubt the two of them would get on quite well.

"Grace," he allowed. Damn him if these Winter half siblings were not nearly as bad as he had supposed them to be.

He liked them, in fact.

Strange, that.

The babe in his arms added a loud sound as if she were agreeing with him. He smiled at her, thinking children were better than cats.

"Would you mind holding her?" Grace asked. "I will return in but a moment."

"Here now," he grumbled. "I am not the child's nurse."

"Of course you are not. But uncles must hold their nieces."

They must? Since when?

She was already on her way out the door of the private family salon, leaving Blade alone with Lady Gwendolyn.

"This is a hell of a thing," he told the infant. "I don't like babes."

She cooed.

"I reckon you aren't bad," he allowed.

Lady Gwendolyn made a new noise, one that sounded rather ecstatic.

He made a sound back at her, and she babbled. For a time, he sat there, the babe in his arms, exchanging noises with her, feeling quite proud of himself whenever Lady Gwendolyn appeared especially enthused. At length, the door to the salon swung open, and he glanced up, expecting to find Grace returning for the child.

Instead, it was none other than the brunette beauty who had been haunting his thoughts ever since he had spotted her wriggling arse in his chamber.

"Lady Felicity," he greeted her, surprised. "I would stand, but I am…"

Hell, he was afraid to move. Lady Gwendolyn was a precious, trusting bundle.

"I see." She hesitated at the threshold. "Forgive me for the interruption, sir. I was searching for my aunt."

He had seen her aunt last night at dinner—a typical society matron who had cast him a look of frigid disapproval. Although Blade had been seated far from Lady Felicity and her chaperone, his eyes had strayed more than once in their direction. In Lady Felicity's direction specifically.

"Do I look as if I harbor aunts to you?" he asked drily, raising a brow.

Her pink tongue flitted over her full lips. "No, but nor do you look as if you harbor infants."

She was not wrong. This was dashed unusual. But for now, he could not stop thinking about her lips. About kissing her. He had been tempted when they had collided the day before. So bloody tempted.

And he was tempted now.

Lady Gwendolyn made another happy sound, reminding him he was not in any condition to kiss anyone. Which was just as well, because he had been sent to Oxfordshire to avoid trouble, damn it. Not create more.

"I don't," he agreed. "This is my…niece."

The word felt strange. A lady was his niece, fancy nib title and all. He had a nephew already, thanks to Dom and Lady Adele. But Colin was a mister, not a lord. Blade had yet to reconcile himself to the fact he was bound by blood to this other half of the Winter family.

Grace chose that moment to appear at Lady Felicity's side on the threshold.

She beamed. "Lady Felicity, I am so happy to find you here. It's quite fortuitous. We need all the players we can find to assemble in the drawing room for a game of hoodman blind in one quarter hour." She turned her enthusiasm upon Blade then. "You as well, brother."

Hoodman blind? A *game*?

"I do not play games," he informed her, suppressing a shudder.

"Of course you do," Grace insisted, crossing the salon and holding out her arms for her daughter. "I must return my little darling to her nurse, and then I shall join you."

"No games," he repeated, the mere thought of engaging in something so frivolous making him want to hide.

"Nonsense." Grace scooped up her daughter. "Were you a good little lady for Uncle Blade?"

His cravat felt too tight. What the devil was going on here? Lusting after a virgin, rescuing a kitten, holding a babe, and now being cozened into playing a game? And he rather missed the cherub, now she'd been taken from his arms.

Hell.

"She hardly made a sound," he gritted, not certain if the question had truly been meant for him. Presumably—the babe could not speak.

But Grace was already moving from the room. He stood belatedly, in deference, remembering himself.

"Come with me, Lady Felicity," Grace said smoothly. "It would not do for your reputation were you to spend so much as a moment in my brother's presence. After that duel…"

Damnation.

Lady Felicity's hazel gaze met his for a brief moment before she turned her attention back to Grace. She followed his half sister out the door. And for the first time in his life, he experienced the stinging rush of shame for what he had done.

Quickly, he banished it.

There was no way in hell he was going to play some silly drawing room game.

MR. BLADE WINTER was not in the drawing room by the time the guests assembled for the game of hoodman blind. Felicity told herself she ought not to be disappointed by his absence. He had informed Lady Aylesford in his cutting way that he did not play games. Why should she have expected him?

It was not as if she wanted to see him or to spend more time with him. No, indeed. It was not as if she had been hoping for the excuse to touch him once more, albeit beneath the perfectly respectable guise of the drawing room entertainment.

Yes it was.

Felicity tamped all such unwanted emotions down, forcing herself to look instead at the eligible gentlemen in attendance. There was Lord Boddington. He had a head of dark hair, kind, brown eyes, and he was the heir to Marquess Worthly.

It hardly mattered that he was not a handsome golden-haired rogue with a dimple that drove her to distraction. Mr.

Blade Winter was altogether unsuitable. Even his name was disreputable, to say nothing of the rest of him. Why, he was part of the Winter family who had been born on the wrong side of the blanket. The Winters who lived in the rookeries and ran a notorious gaming hell along with all manner of criminal enterprises.

Lady Emilia Winter, as the hostess, began speaking, explaining the rules of the game. A blindfold would be tied around the eyes of one person. That person would be spun about in a circle, then have to go about the drawing room as the other players attempted to avoid him or her. When the person who was "it" caught someone, they had to guess their identity.

"Who shall go first?" she asked.

"I will," announced the Duchess of Coventry.

The blindfold was placed on her, the duchess was spun about, and she began searching the chamber. Fortunately for her, the first person she caught was her husband, the duke, who stood still for her comical exploration of his person, which began with his nose.

"Coventry," she guessed with a grin in no time.

Her laughing husband admitted she was correct, and then it was Coventry's turn to be blindfolded. The festivities proceeded for some time, Felicity mildly entertained as the various players took their turns. At last, Lady Aylesford caught Felicity and guessed correctly, much to Felicity's consternation.

She held still as the blindfold was placed over her eyes and she was spun until she was so dizzy she stumbled. *Good heavens*, for the second time in as many days, she was going to fall and make a complete fool of herself. And just when she had to make the best impression.

When she was desperate.

She attempted to regain her balance and composure, but both had swung wildly in the wrong direction. Her arms stretched before her, waving in windmill fashion. It was too much. After attempting to take a frantic step forward, her slipper caught in the hem of her gown.

And then, she was hurtling forward.

Until she wasn't.

She landed against a body. Masculine, warm, and firm. Her hands clutched at the lapels of a gentleman's coat. With her eyes blindfolded, she felt so completely at a disadvantage. But the rest of her senses were more alive than ever.

A scent reached her. The hands that were on her upper arms felt...familiar.

Citrus, musk, man.

She gasped as recognition dawned. But how could it be? He had not even been in the drawing room when the blindfold had been tied around her eyes. Had he?

"You have been caught, Lady Felicity," said a female voice.

Laughter accompanied her call from various ends of the room.

Still, the hands on her would not release Felicity. She had indeed been caught, and she feared she knew by whom. Her pounding heart and the fierce reaction burning through her told her exactly who it was.

She ought to guess and simply forfeit the blindfold. Put an end to this foolish game and reckless desire to keep touching Mr. Blade Winter. He was the last sort of man she should want. There was no future for her with a man like him. He was the sort who ruined ladies. And had not Lady Aylesford told her all about the duel he had so recently fought? Over a married lady, no less.

The reminder caused a new burst of resentment to unfurl

within her. She ought to push him away. To stomp on his foot.

Instead, a wicked idea blossomed.

She could touch him as she pleased, and he could do nothing to stop her. He could not tease her, say a word, or display his maddening grin. He could not touch her in return, beyond steadying her as he had done.

"I am no longer in danger of falling," she told him crisply. "Thank you."

With more of a delay than was necessary or proper, he slowly released his gentle grip on her arms. There. Mayhap if he was no longer touching her, the rushing in her ears would stop and her heart would resume its normal, sedate pace instead of running on at a distracted gallop.

Her fingertips glided over his coat, finding his broad shoulders and skimming across them. "Your shoulders are quite small," she announced to the chamber. "Why, if you were not wearing a gentleman's coat, I should have thought you a lady."

It was difficult indeed to keep the smile from her lips as she uttered the last.

He made a snorting sound but said nothing.

"You must be a young man," she guessed next, running her hands down his arms.

In truth, touching him thus was intoxicating. Her heart had only sped up its pace. It was as if no one else existed in the drawing room beyond the two of them. Her lips tingled, and she wondered if his brilliant gaze was upon them. Somehow, instinctively, she knew it was. She ran her tongue over her lower lip.

He made another sound. Not a snort this time.

She had his attention.

Felicity reached his hands. Strong hands, big hands, work-roughened fingertips. Yes, this was him. Had she had any doubt, here was her proof. So, too, in the heat that slid through her. She recognized him. Her body recognized him. But another, deeper part of her did as well.

Her breath caught as his fingers unexpectedly linked with hers, but then she forced herself to continue as if she were unaffected. It would not do to allow him to see how much his nearness undid her.

"Small, dainty hands," she said, continuing her campaign.

His fingers tightened on hers in warning.

She suppressed a smile of triumph, realizing she could not guess him to be any of the ladies in attendance lest she offer them the insult of suggesting they possessed the same muscled bearing as Mr. Winter.

Felicity attempted to tug her hands free, but he held her in his steady grasp, their fingers tangled.

"Come on then," someone called. "Make your guess, Lady Felicity."

"Who do you suppose the *lady* in question can be?" chortled yet another guest.

He gave her fingers another warning squeeze, as if to suggest he intended to get even with her following the game. She had no doubt he would try, and she was not entirely certain she would be sorry for it, though the rational part of her knew she must keep her distance. He was a rogue. A scoundrel.

Not husband material.

And she most definitely needed a husband.

But first, what was the matter with indulging in temptation?

"I am not certain," she announced to the group of revelers, finally succeeding in removing her hands from his grasp. "Perhaps a bit more of an inspection."

Titters met her words.

What had she expected? She was the sole one amongst them who was blindfolded. But she had pretense on her side, and she was enjoying the freedom to explore Mr. Blade Winter's form, all while taunting him.

The upper hand was hers, at least for the next five minutes.

And she intended to enjoy it while she could.

She reached up, settling her hands on his jaw. The subtle prickle of his whiskers was a delightful abrasion against her seeking palms. She barely suppressed a shiver of awareness as she caressed along those sharp lines. She could not resist trailing her fingers over his lips next.

His breath coasted over her skin. His lips were soft, supple. She inhaled swiftly, the sound maddeningly sharp and loud in the sudden quiet of the drawing room. She had to put an end to this farce. It was affecting her far too much.

She stopped touching him. "Mr. Winter."

"Excellent guess." The wry baritone was familiar.

He was still near enough. A frisson swept down her spine. Her heightened senses knew the moment he stepped closer, reaching behind her to untie the knot on her blindfold. When it was removed, she blinked at the sudden brightness.

He was watching her with an expression she rather fancied a fox would wear before he caught his prey. He raised a golden brow, looking sinfully handsome.

"Tie the blindfold on me, then," he told her, holding out the silken tie.

She took it from him, their fingers brushing. His gaze promised retribution. But she could not summon a modicum of regret.

Chapter Four

"*My* darling Mrs. Winter." Devereaux Winter could not keep the smile from his lips as he greeted his beloved wife Emilia that evening in their chamber.

She was holding their infant son, Charles, in her arms, and she had never been more beautiful. Although theirs had begun as a marriage of convenience, it had quickly turned into an affair of the heart. Each day, he loved her more than the last. He was besotted with his wife, and he did not care who knew it.

"My love," she said softly. "I was just holding him before taking him to the nursery. He is sleeping quite soundly, but I find myself hesitant to relinquish him, as always."

She was a wonderful mama to their son. But then, he had known she would be. Gratitude swept over him as he gazed upon mother and child. His heart was so damned full.

Dev crossed the chamber and leaned down to bestow a kiss on first Emilia's lips and then Charles's head, taking care not to wake the sleeping babe. "There is my strong lad. Growing larger every day."

Emilia's smile was tender. "He has his papa's size. Just a few months old and already so strapping."

Dev was an immense man, he knew, with his own father's broad shoulders and towering height. Those traits had been what made it apparent the bastard Winters—Dominic, Devil,

Blade, Demon, Gavin, and Genevieve—shared a sire with him. Genevieve was tall for a lady, much like his sister Pru.

"Are you enjoying being here at Abingdon Hall for another Christmastide, darling?" he asked, though he knew the answer.

Last year's country house party had become an annual tradition. The only difference was that last year, their primary aim had been to see his younger sisters happily married. Miraculously—and despite some scandal—they had succeeded. Each of his sisters was wed and happier than he could have hoped.

"I adore being here, as you know," Emilia told him softly. "I am so pleased you invited your brothers and sister."

"Half brothers and half sister," he reminded her. Though in truth, what had begun as an acrimonious relationship between himself and the formerly secret offspring of his father had transitioned into something different.

He almost *liked* them.

Almost.

"Family," she returned, "any way you say it."

His wife—who possessed the heart of an angel—had been the architect of the thawing of the ice between himself and the bastard Winters. His fierce sense of family—once relegated to Emilia, their child, and his sisters and their families—had expanded. But then, Emilia had enlarged his life in so many other ways, he was hardly surprised by this latest feather in her cap.

"Family," he agreed, unable to resist giving her tempting lips another kiss.

This one lingered. And deepened. She made a sweet, breathy sigh that undid him.

Dev forced himself to recall she was holding Charles and removed his lips from hers. "I warned Blade he is not to cause any trouble. If you hear word of any wrongdoing, I will toss him out on his arse."

When Emilia had initially suggested they invite the other half of the Winter family—the half that hailed from the rookeries—to their country house party, he had been dubious. But Dom and Devil had married and settled down, and he had reluctantly decided to give the rest of them a chance as well.

Dom and Devil were also having babes, which meant they were not able to travel to Oxfordshire. Which also meant Dev was being saddled with the tremendous task of keeping his unruly half siblings in order.

"He will behave himself, I am certain," Emilia said, stroking their son's cheek, an expression stealing over her lovely face he knew too well. "I saw the way he has been watching Lady Felicity Hughes."

"Emilia," he said in a tone of mock warning. "Do not think it."

"Some matchmaking could be just the thing to liven up this house party." She flashed him a mischievous grin. "Besides, would you not like to see *all* your siblings happily settled?"

He groaned. "You did quite well last year, but this particular company of Winters is not at all the same."

She raised a brow. "I beg to differ. You are Winters. Though you may have had vastly different upbringings, there is much in each of you that is the same. Not just your uncommon height and fierce sense of family."

"Hmm." He was not convinced. "You cannot be thinking of matching Lady Felicity with Blade. He just fought a duel and nearly killed the Earl of Penhurst. Lady Felicity is far too proper for a man of his sort."

"Her aunt hinted that she must make a match, and soon.

There are two younger sisters who must also have their come outs. Grace told me she sensed something between Lady Felicity and Blade. She would aid me in matchmaking, I should think."

"Emilia." He tried to give her a disapproving frown, but how could he when she looked so damned beautiful, holding their son?

"You missed hoodman's blind this afternoon," she continued, her mind already decided. "If you had seen the way the two of them looked at each other, you would understand."

He sighed. "I hate hoodman blind." Then he kissed her mouth again. "But I love you."

She smiled against his lips. "I love you, too. I shall take Charles to the nursery, and when I return, I will show you just how much."

He already knew, but he was not about to argue. One more quick kiss, this one chaste, before he straightened. "Fair enough, but allow me to escort you, Mrs. Winter."

Her smile deepened. "If you insist, Mr. Winter. I did miss you this evening when you were playing host to the gentlemen."

"I missed you more," he said.

Together, they took their sleeping son to the nursery.

HOODMAN BLIND.

A damned drawing room game.

Blade was still disgusted with himself the next morning when he left the breakfast room. Ordinarily, a solid rasher of bacon, a plate of eggs, and some fruit was enough to please him. When a man knew what it was like to go hungry, he appreciated every meal he was given. But not even a belly full of excellent food could quell the irritation lurking within him.

There was no excuse for what he had done yesterday, no reason he had gone to the drawing room at all. Save one.

Her.

He had mingled with the other revelers all because he had known Lady Felicity would be there. And when she had been blindfolded, he had made certain he was the one with whom she came into contact first. She was not bloody well touching anyone else on his watch.

At least Demon, Gavin, and Genevieve were due to arrive soon, thank Christ. Mayhap he could distract himself with them. Regain his sanity. If indeed he possessed any.

He was questioning it more and more with each passing hour.

"There you are, Mr. Winter!"

He turned on his heel to find his hostess and sister-in-law, Lady Emilia Winter, approaching him. Despite the fact she was an aristocrat, daughter to a duke, she had been welcoming and friendly. Rather in the fashion of Dom's and Devil's wives.

Mayhap not all aristocratic ladies were awful.

He dismissed the notion. It hardly mattered anyway. It was not as if he were going to court Lady Felicity. *Laughable!* He had no need for a wife. There was an endless parade of petticoats waiting to share his bed. And take a wife? *Ha! Never.*

He bowed, astonished at himself. He was playing the gentleman with ease these days. "My lady. How may I be of service?"

"I was on my way to the yellow salon to fetch my sewing, but I also need to see to the entertainments planned for this evening. Do you think you might fetch it for me?" She smiled sweetly as she asked the question.

Christ. Did she not have a house filled with servants for such matters?

Yes, she did. But he was a guest. And damn it, although fetching *sewing* rankled, at least it would give him something to do. Something useful. Something that did not involve giving in to his base urges and seeking out the maddening Lady Felicity.

The minx had called his shoulders *small* and his hands *dainty.* His outrage at the time had been diminished by the extreme desire her nearness and slow, innocent caresses had inspired. Impertinent baggage.

"I would be more than happy to, Lady Emilia," he said, forcing thoughts of *her* from his mind once more.

Abingdon House was a monstrous affair, but he had been in the yellow salon—it was where he had been duped into holding an infant the day before. He could find it on his own well enough.

"Thank you, Blade." His half brother's wife beamed. "Please do call me Emilia. We are family."

Family. Still a strange notion, connected to these Winters. He still felt like a fish plucked from a river, suddenly thrust into a strange, unfamiliar world.

He blinked. "It would be my honor."

His honor? *Hell.* Since when did a man born in the depths of the rookeries speak thus? Since when did *Blade* say such fucking tripe? Being in the monkery was making him spoony. The sooner he returned to London and this cursed house party was over, the better.

He bowed and made haste before he started dancing a cotillion or holding a quizzing glass to his eye. For a house that was filled with guests, the walk to the yellow salon was surprisingly bereft of any others.

Which was why, when he crossed the threshold of that

chamber and found someone else within, he was taken aback. Initially by the presence of another. And then because of the identity of the room's other occupant.

Her.

As if conjured from his tortured imaginings, Lady Felicity Hughes stood in the center of the room. Though her back was to him, he would recognize her anywhere. Warmth swept over him, landing in his groin. She was once more all ethereal elegance, dressed in a pale-yellow gown, her chestnut curls captured in a chignon. She had not realized he had entered the room, and he took a moment to admire her.

Just one.

Then he spoke, because now that he had her where he wanted her, how could he deny himself the opportunity to have his revenge upon her for the little game she had played at his expense the day before?

"Lady Felicity."

She spun about on a shriek, hand flying over her heart, eyes wide. She had been holding a book in her hands, and the volume flew across the carpet, landing with a thud. He had truly given her a fright.

Blade grinned at her, unrepentant, and sauntered deeper into the room. "Do try to cease hollering. I would hate for the company to come racing here, thinking I have ravished you."

"Mr. Winter! What are you doing here?"

Her cheeks had turned that delicious shade of pink he had come to know and enjoy. Her tone was one of chastisement. He wanted to kiss her breathless.

"I came to fetch our hostess's sewing, at her request." He bent down to retrieve the book she had flung when he had given her a start. "What are *you* doing here?"

"Give that to me," she said, instead of answering his question.

He could not deny her defensiveness about the thin, leather-bound volume intrigued him.

"Don't think I will," he told her, glancing down at the unassuming cover.

She reached for it, her cheeks growing redder still.

This was not the distraction he had sought, but it was an even better one. His grin deepening, he held the book over her head, quite out of reach. There were two benefits to having been born the bastard of old man Winter. His height was one, his siblings the other.

"Mr. Winter, please."

He liked the way she begged. It brought to mind other, more sinful means of begging. "Please what, Lady Felicity? I am afraid you will have to elaborate."

She jumped, the action making her breasts bounce delightfully.

Scoundrel that he was, he held the book higher and kept his stare riveted. Her hazel eyes were rimmed with dark gray, her lashes long. *Damn*, but she was beautiful. And her irritation only enhanced her loveliness.

If only he was not meant to stay out of trouble.

"The book is not mine, and I have been tasked with returning it to its true owner." She leapt again, reaching for the book.

This time, she lost her balance. She fell forward, colliding with his chest. He caught her to him with his free arm, anchoring her lush body to his. Nothing but feminine curves and prickly outrage and heat emerging from her. Along with the scent of jasmine.

"Do you know what I think, Lady Felicity?" he asked, dipping his head so their faces were near, as if he were imparting a secret.

Or about to kiss her tempting lips.

Said lips parted. "Mr. Winter."

But the bite was gone from her tone. Her stare dipped to his mouth.

"Yes, darling?" he teased.

Blade could not help himself. Supposed to stay away from trouble or not, trouble was currently in his arms, and he had no intention of letting her go so easily.

"You are being insufferably forward. No gentleman would act in such a disreputable fashion." She blinked, her gaze returning to his at last. "Nor have I given you leave to speak to me with such familiarity. I am *not* your darling."

"I never claimed to be a gentleman, Lady Felicity." His hand traveled of its own volition, smoothing around her waist as he eased his hold on her, finding the curve of her lower back, then tracing her spine higher. Everywhere he touched her, he felt the sizzle of awareness between them in a way he never had before.

Not with any other woman.

He truly needed to get back to London. What was it about bloody Oxfordshire that was rotting his mind?

"Your actions certainly support that." Her tone was cool, her raised brow a reproach.

Was she speaking of the duel? *Hell.* Curse Grace and her wagging tongue to perdition.

"The countess suggested she had an understanding with her husband. The earl informed me otherwise. Honor had to be satisfied." Blade shrugged as if he had not a care. "I was aiming to miss, but the fool moved. It was his fault."

"You are scandalous, Mr. Winter. I should not know you."

But although she said the words, her expression—and the way her body remained fitted to his—suggested she did not object nearly as much as she protested.

He lowered his head another fraction, all while keeping the book held aloft. "But you want to know me, Lady Felicity. Admit it."

Her tongue darted out to sweep over the fullness of her lower lip. "I shall admit no such thing. To do so would be ruinous, and I am here to make a match. To find a husband."

Well, proper fuck.

That was not what he wanted to hear, though he supposed it should not come as a surprise. Was not every eligible lady in London marriage-minded? And should not a lady with a father who was so inept at the green baize, younger sisters awaiting their uncertain futures, be all the more in search of a husband?

"Husbands are deadly boring," he told her anyway.

Partly because they were. And no one knew that better than Blade, who had found himself entertaining more than his fair share of wives who wanted nothing to do with their husbands. But also partly because the notion of Lady Felicity getting leg-shackled to some pathetic lord irritated the devil out of him.

"Not when your sisters' futures depend upon them," she countered.

There it was. Proof that she needed to marry—and well— for the sake of the ladies who would follow in her footsteps. He ought to release her. Give her the stupid book. Step away. Never again think of being near her.

She was a *virgin*, for God's sake. A lady. And though he had bedded his fair share of those, this one was different.

It was despicable.

He was despicable.

"Why not enjoy yourself before you sell your body and soul to save your sisters?" he found himself asking.

Her nostrils flared. Her body stiffened. "I am not a

lightskirt, Mr. Winter. I am selling nothing. I intend to marry, and soon. That is what is expected of me, and that is what is proper."

What a cursed shame, that a woman as lively and lovely as Lady Felicity should find herself desperate to marry. Adhering to nonsensical societal rules. Curtseying her way into a dismal future. Sacrificing herself because her father was a terrible gambler who did not know one more turn of the cards or roll of the dice would only bleed him drier.

"Is it proper for us to be this close just now?" he taunted, sweeping his hand higher.

He found the nape of her neck, softer than silk, and warm. So warm. So inviting. His fingers plunged into her chignon.

"No," she whispered, her lips falling open. "It is most improper."

Her gaze dipped back to his mouth.

If she had exerted a hint of pressure to push him away, he would have allowed her to go. As it was, he was not holding her to him with any strength. There was nothing but the undeniable desire burning hot and bright between them that kept her where she was.

"Mayhap you ought to move, then." As he delivered the challenge, he caressed her neck with his thumb. Slow, steady swirls over her skin.

And she moved, it was true.

But not away from him.

In the next breath, she tugged his head down to hers and their mouths met at last.

Chapter Five

*A*T LAST.

Felicity felt as if she had waited an entire lifetime for this man's lips on hers. Which was ludicrous, because she had only met him a scant few days ago. She scarcely knew him. And yet, she could not shake the sensation, deep and ingrained, that there was something inevitable about him. About this moment. About this kiss.

Not her first.

She had kissed a handful of gentlemen before. No easy feat, with watchful chaperones and the care she took with her reputation. But she had kissed several of her suitors. Each of them had left her feeling pleasant but hardly transformed.

None of those kisses compared to this one.

Blade Winter was a rogue and she knew it, but he kissed like an angel.

A wicked angel.

His lips moved over hers, parting them, his tongue slipping inside her mouth. He tasted like pineapple. He must have sampled one of the pineapples from the Abingdon House orangery at breakfast. Such sweetness, mingled with temptation.

She should stop this. Push him away. He held her as gently as if she were Sèvres porcelain. Felicity knew without bothering to try that she could slip away with ease. That was the problem. She did not *want* to slip away. She had been waiting all her life for this, for *him*.

Or so it seemed as his mouth worshiped hers.

She forgot about reaching for the naughty book that belonged to Lady Aylesford, which she had been tasked with rescuing from the salon by the lady herself. Forgot about propriety, all the reasons why she should be running as far from this room and this man as possible. All she could think about, all she could feel, all she wanted, was Blade Winter's kiss.

Her arms wound around his neck. She pressed her body to his in shameless fashion. Hungering for him. Longing for him, quite desperately. Not even common sense or the fear of her future could stop her now. His lips were too potent. His touch on her nape—that incendiary graze of his thumb pad over her skin—enough to drive her mad.

She inhaled, and all she breathed was him. Decadent, forbidden, everything she should not want. Everything she wanted anyway.

Somewhere, a thump sounded.

The book, mayhap?

She should put an end to the kiss and fetch it. Certainly she ought to remember she had come to this country house party with one purpose in mind: to find herself a husband.

But then, his taunting, tempting words came back to her.

Why not enjoy yourself before you sell your body and soul to save your sisters?

She could not summon a single argument against his query just now, with his lips moving over hers. Melding to hers. Possessing hers. *Good heavens*, he kissed with such mastery, she could well understand why a married woman would go chasing after him.

Why not enjoy herself, just for a moment? Just for this

kiss?

He kissed the corners of her mouth, then nipped her lower lip between his teeth. A startled moan tore from her. He was fierce. Savage. Wild.

Everything she should not want.

Everything she wanted anyway.

"You taste so bloody sweet." He traced the sting of his tender bites with his tongue. "Damn it, I could kiss you all day."

Yes, if you please.

But that was wrong. She could not kiss him all day. Or at all. Indeed, she had to stop this dangerous nonsense at once. And she would, just as soon as he…

"Oh," she whispered as his knowing mouth traveled from hers at last, finding her throat. Latching on to the place where her heart beat so frantically. Sucking. Licking.

Her knees trembled.

She clutched him.

This was… No kiss had ever been so… She had no words. None.

He kissed his way to her ear, his hot breath grazing her, making her shiver. And then he kissed the space behind it, his tongue roaming over the hollow she had never realized was so sensitive until this moment. This time, her knees did not just tremble. They turned to pudding. She would have collapsed had he not caught her with a strong arm around the waist, drawing her more firmly against him.

So firmly the undeniable ridge of his manhood pressed into her belly. Felicity was not entirely ignorant—she had paged through the secret book Lady Aylesford had requested she retrieve. And it had been…informative. Interesting.

Not nearly as interesting as Blade Winter's hard, uncompromising body pressed to hers.

"Tell me to stop," he said against her throat, before his wicked mouth traveled lower. Across her décolletage, the exposed portion of her bosom. "Say the word, darling."

She should.

But then he tugged at her gown and stays. One strong movement, and her breasts popped free. Bared for him. She had never been so vulnerable, so exposed. And yet, she had never felt more alive.

His lips moved over her, inciting more passion. More pleasure. And when he sucked her nipple into his mouth, she cried out, her back arching, her body seeking. It was as if a cord ran between her breast and her core. He flicked his tongue over her nipple, making her ache in a wonderful, new way.

He lapped at her, and it was wicked. She ought to look away. To stop him. But the sight of his handsome face nestled so near to her breast, his mouth on her, was unutterably pleasurable. Sinful. Delicious.

She had never felt more alive than she did in this moment, in this scandalous man's arms.

All wrong.

So right.

He moved to her other breast, delivering the same sweet torture.

Felicity tried to remind herself of the necessity that she maintain her reputation. That she find a proper husband. One with enough wealth to make her sisters' debuts possible. A husband who was the complete opposite of this rough-hewn rogue who fought duels with cuckolded husbands, whose kisses would surely lead to worse sin.

But none of these reminders rendered the pleasure he wrung from her any less potent. His mouth upon her made bliss sear her straight to her toes.

Just as she was beginning to lose complete control, and with it any ability to keep from ruining herself, however, he stopped. His head lifted, and with one violent tug that bespoke his experience in such matters, he pulled her bodice back into place.

Her heart was pounding with so much force, she swore he could likely hear it.

"Don't suppose that was proper, was it?" he murmured, smirking at her.

Her cheeks went hot. *Every* part of her went hot. His dimple returned, mocking her. He was so handsome, and she had just allowed him to take shocking liberties. The sort she had never permitted another gentleman. The sort that were not just ruinous for her reputation, but deadly. If anyone were to have walked in upon them, she would have had to retire from polite society.

And then where would Esme and Cassandra be?

"You are a scoundrel, sir."

He shrugged. "Never claimed to be a saint."

"There is a vast difference between a saint and a scoundrel," she pointed out, her voice trembling.

She had to retrieve the blasted book, remove herself from this chamber, and make sure she was never alone with him again. He was too tempting. Too adept at seduction. She wondered how many other ladies he had kissed and wooed, and her stomach clenched.

He was a rakehell. Undoubtedly, his conquests were legion. According to Lady Aylesford, Blade Winter was quite sought after despite his humble upbringing in the rookery.

Had he made any of them feel the way he had made her feel? Jealousy she had no right to entertain rose, strong and insistent, along with the need for self-preservation.

He watched her, not saying a word, that blue gaze of his

positively scorching. She was trapped in it. Ensnared as surely as she had been by his kisses and his wicked, wicked mouth.

"Have you nothing to say for yourself?" she demanded, infuriated with him, with herself.

How could she have been so foolish? So reckless? So desperately wanton?

His grin deepened, unrepentant. "What would you have me say, darling? I won't apologize for pleasuring you. I heard nary a complaint when my mouth was on your—"

"That is enough, Mr. Winter," she bit out, interrupting him lest he finish his sentence and turn her to flame.

"I told you to tell me to stop. And yet, you did not. Nary a hint of protest. If anything, you were quite…welcoming."

So he had. And so she had not. And…curse him, she had been welcoming in a fashion most unbecoming of a lady, it was true. Particularly an unwed lady. And most especially an unwed lady desperate to land herself a husband.

She huffed out a breath. "I have no wish to argue with you, Mr. Winter."

"Because you would lose."

His quick, smug retort made her long to box his ears. And then kiss him some more.

Drat.

Now where had that thought come from?

Felicity squared her shoulders, preparing for further battle. "On the contrary, sir. I am confident I would win. However, I have no wish to argue with you because I need to do what I promised. The owner of the book is eagerly awaiting its return, and I can hardly afford to be caught alone with someone such as yourself."

His grin slowly faded. "Someone such as myself, Lady Felicity? And what is someone such as myself? Do tell."

"Someone…" She searched for the word she wanted, but

it felt like an insult. Her lips would not form it, not after his had just been upon them.

"Someone common," he elaborated for her. "Someone baseborn. A scoundrel, a rogue, a rookery thief. An assassin. A bastard."

She hated the way those aspersions left his tongue with ease. She hated even more that she had been about to say some of them. That she had said some of them.

But there was one which stood out, one she had never thought in conjunction with him.

"A-are you an assassin?" she asked haltingly.

This beautiful man—a murderer? She could hardly make the connection.

He inclined his head. "I was. Now I work to keep Winter family interests safe by encouraging all the cheats, thieves, and liars to stay honorable in other, painful ways. The East End isn't a ballroom, my lady. We do not bow and curtsy. We fight for everything we have, and then when we have it, we do everything we can to defend what is ours."

He had been an assassin. She felt lightheaded. Had he...killed?

Her gaze dropped to his hands. So strong, those long fingers tempting and yet mayhap dangerous. The inking of the dagger on the top of his hand taunted her. It was situated between his thumb and forefinger, black and bold and feral.

She shivered against her will.

"Fearful now, darling?" he asked, leaning toward her and lowering his head so their lips almost grazed once more. "You need not be. I protect my family's holdings from enemies. Not from frivolous virgins who lower themselves to kissing a commoner."

"Is that the way all the ladies you seduce think of you?" she asked before she could think better of the question. "That you are a commoner? That they are your betters?"

The moment they fled her lips, she wished she could call the questions back.

The other ladies—she must not think of them. Moreover, there was something of far greater import she must force herself to think of. Mr. Blade Winter was far more dangerous than she had supposed.

"Darling, I hate to tell you, but *you* are the one who seduced *me*," he said, catching her chin in a gentle grip, tilting her face up to meet his.

How dare he suggest such a thing?

"You are wrong, Mr. Winter."

"Mmm. Did you not kiss me first?"

Good heavens. He was correct. She *had* been the one who had kissed him first. What had she been thinking? Moreover, what was she doing, lingering with him now, putting her reputation in increasing danger with each passing moment?

She pushed away from him at once and knelt, searching for the book he had dropped to the carpets. It had fallen on its spine. And, as fortune would have it—mayhap misfortune, in this instance—the engraving upon the opened pages was positively indecent. She gaped at it.

Was the gentleman truly beneath the lady's raised skirts with his head between her thighs?

"My, what have you been reading, darling?"

The wry question, issued in Blade Winter's deep, delicious baritone, shook her from her momentary shock. Face heating anew, she retrieved the volume and snapped it closed before rising to her feet.

"I told you, sir, that it is not mine. Nor have I been reading it. I was merely asked to fetch the forgotten volume and return it to its rightful owner," she said, avoiding his gaze, all too aware of her heated cheeks. And ears. Heavens, even her eyebrows were likely ablaze at this point.

What manner of scandalous treatise had Lady Aylesford required her to retrieve? The viscountess had said the book was a secret matter, and that Felicity should take care not to allow anyone else to see her carrying it about. But she had not said it was…lewd.

Bawdy.

Despicably sinful.

Wrongly intriguing.

Against her will, she wanted to carry the book to her chamber and page through it herself without Mr. Blade Winter's scrutiny upon her.

"Return it to its rightful owner," Mr. Winter repeated, his tone mocking. "Of course, my lady."

He did not believe her.

She ground her jaws. "It is not mine, if that is what you suggest."

He shrugged. "I suggest nothing. However, you are the only one I see attempting to retrieve the book in question."

He was not wrong about that. However…

"You are the only one I see attempting to fetch our hostess's sewing," she countered. "It is odd indeed for a gentleman such as yourself to retrieve such a thing. Why not a servant?"

"That is what I want to know," he grumbled.

And she believed him. He may be many things, Mr. Blade Winter, but it did not appear that liar was amongst the many appellations which could be applied to him.

"Lady Emilia requested you fetch her sewing from this salon," Felicity said, repeating his earlier claim.

"Do I look like the sort of man who goes about searching for sewing, for Christ's sake?" he asked.

No, he did not. Instead, he looked like the sort of man who could make a lady bend to his whims with a mere grin.

He looked like temptation incarnate. The sort of man every lady was sternly warned to avoid by her chaperones prior to her comeout. And every day thereafter.

"Of course not." She frowned at him, understanding beginning to dawn upon her. "But Lady Emilia sent you here to this salon, yes?"

He nodded.

"And someone else also sent me here to fetch her book," she said, deliberately keeping Lady Aylesford's name out of their discussion.

"Do you know what I think, Lady Felicity?"

She blinked at him, flustered, confused, holding the book to her still-racing heart. "What is it that you think, Mr. Winter?"

"I think the book is yours."

"It is not!" she denied hotly.

"Hmm," was all he said.

The vexing, infuriatingly handsome man.

"It is not mine," she denied once more.

"Nor is the sewing mine," he allowed. "Have you seen it anywhere?"

"I was looking for the book." And then, she had been looking at him. Only him. He had absorbed every last modicum of her attention.

"I shall search for it, then." His full lips pursed.

God, how she wanted to feel those lips against hers once more.

It was a sin.

And she wanted it anyway.

"Very well," she agreed. "And I shall return this book to its owner."

She forced herself to dip into a curtsy. "I bid you good day, Mr. Winter."

He bowed, the action perfunctory. Not quite elegant, and somehow mocking in true Blade Winter fashion. He was not a man who prized formality or society. Nor, she suspected, would he ever be.

"And I bid you a good morning, my lady Felicity," he returned. "The day is young. Do think about what I said, will you not?"

She knew without bothering to ask exactly what he meant.

Why not enjoy yourself before you sell your body and soul to save your sisters?

She raced from the chamber, leaving the temptation of Mr. Blade Winter behind.

For now.

"It was terribly wicked of you to ask Lady Felicity to retrieve *The Tale of Love* from the yellow salon, darling."

Grace smiled at her handsome husband Rand, Viscount Aylesford, as they prepared for dinner that evening. "I thought you did not mind when I am wicked."

His gaze heated. "You know I do not." He drew her to him, kissing her soundly. "When it is the two of us, you may be as wicked as you choose. But that book is not the sort of literature one ought to put into the hands of an innocent."

"My sisters and I all read it before we were wed," she pointed out, then pulled his handsome head back to hers for another meeting of lips.

Her husband's gaze was on her lips. "Yes, but you are all Winter ladies."

She raised a brow. "And what does that mean, Lord Aylesford, *Winter ladies*?"

He kissed the tip of her nose affectionately, melting any irritation she may have felt. "Only that you are originals. Lady Felicity, I daresay, has not all your forward-thinking natures."

Mayhap, but Grace rather liked Lady Felicity Hughes. There was something about her that was earnest, vulnerable, and yet also an underlying hint of an independent nature Grace could wholeheartedly applaud. Besides, now that she was happily married herself, she could not resist the urge to play matchmaker.

She nuzzled Rand's cheek with hers, inhaling deeply of his delectable scent. "I like her for Blade."

"*Blade Winter?*" Her husband's mouth traveled to her throat, finding a place that drove her mad.

That was one of the excellent things about reforming an arrogant rake—he knew how to bring her to her knees. And as a husband, he was loyal to a fault. He loved her unconditionally, and he loved her family as well. Even the bastards who had so recently appeared, fresh from the East End and speaking in flash. She loved him for his open heart all the more.

Belatedly, she recalled Rand had asked her a question. "Do you know any other gentlemen named Blade?"

Rand nibbled on her collarbone. "Mmm. Cannot be his Christian name, do you think?"

Her fingers explored the broad expanse of her husband's shoulders through his coat. "If it is not, I shall fully expect Lady Felicity to divulge the truth when they marry. You should have seen the way he held our sweet little angel. There is far more to him than meets the eye, and Lady Felicity is stronger than she seems, with all her pale gowns."

Her husband's tongue flicked over the hollow where her pulse pounded, giving away the effect he had upon her. "Bold of you, darling. They appear quite opposite. An ominous scoundrel with a penchant for knives and a name to match, coupled with a diamond of the first water?"

"Nobility and commoners can get on together quite well; one need only to look at the two of us to see that," she said, gasping as he deftly tugged down her bodice, making her nipples pop free. "My lord, we must attend dinner."

"Must we?" He kissed his way down the slope of her breast. "I am famished, it is true, but only for you."

When his knowing mouth found her nipple and lapped at the tender bud, she could not stifle her moan of appreciation. "Perhaps we could cry off dinner after all."

Chapter Six

"IF YOU ASK me, Dom expecting us all to wallow in the monkery is spoony," Gavin grumbled. "I could have won two prizefights in the time it took us to rumble here in a carriage. How the hell am I to keep up with my sparring?"

"Especially with the Winters and all the other nibs." Genevieve tilted her head, eying the trunk of the tree where she intended to throw her blade from beneath the brim of her hat. "At least we can throw knives here. Damned difficult to do at The Devil's Spawn without some drunken shite wandering past and taking a blade to the ear."

It had happened once. Gen had sliced a portion of Lord Hildebrand's earlobe when he had inadvertently wandered into one of their knife-tossing competitions. A surprising amount of blood had ensued for a small wound. To say nothing of the manner in which old Lord Hildebrand had pissed in his breeches…

"You are taking too long, Gen," Demon complained. "It's sodding cold out here. My fingers will freeze before you make your throw."

"Aye, and then how will you lift all the ladies' skirts?" Gavin chortled.

Blade watched his siblings, gathered beneath a copse of winter-barren trees, a familiar sense of belonging sliding through him. They had arrived that morning. Thank bloody fuck, because Blade could ill afford to go about kissing Lady Felicity Hughes senseless in the yellow salon for the second day in a row.

The thought of Lady Felicity—and her sweet lips—sent heat flaring through him in direct opposition to the frigid December day.

"Mayhap I'll just make all the birds hold their skirts," Demon suggested with a rakehell's grin. "Ready access to whatever I need, and they do all the work for me. Fair enough with all the pleasure I give them."

"Spare us the disgusting particulars before I retch." Gen snorted. "Don't know why they're all so eager for you to trick them out of their petticoats and fleece them."

"They aren't," Blade added his voice to the good-natured banter. It was better than wallowing in unwanted thoughts about Lady Felicity. "He has to get them tap-hackled first."

"Eh, if we need advice on how *not* to impress a lady, we will ask you," Gavin told him. "Fought any duels since you arrived?"

"Run bare-arsed down the halls to escape an angry husband?" Gen asked, snickering.

"Lady Penhurst sends her love," Demon offered.

Well, bloody hell. He supposed he deserved that. But the reminder of his folly nettled. Had he expected any less from his siblings? No. Demon, Genevieve, and Gavin were a cutthroat trio if ever there was one.

"Throw the damned blade, Gen," he growled at his sister.

His siblings laughed. But just as Gen was about to throw her dagger at last, Demon issued a feigned sneeze that was loud enough to be overheard back in East London.

The weapon flew from her fingers, missing the tree trunk she had been aiming for and hurtling wide, catapulting into the thick forest. A cry rose, almost instantly. Feminine.

Familiar.

Lady Felicity.

Blade's mouth went dry. His booted feet were moving before his mind could make sense of what had just happened. He was tearing through the sticks and thin winter undergrowth, racing to where the sound of her cry had emerged. Downhill, as it turned out. He and his siblings had been on a ridge that was quite deceptive, given the subtle flare of the land and the sheer number of trees.

He slid and slipped on a mixture of snow and ice that blanketed the ground as he spotted a felled form. Dark hair, pastel skirts, and a pale cloak trimmed with fur caught his attention.

Good God, it was her.

And she was lying on the ground.

Terror crept into his heart. Had Gen's blade hit her?

"Lady Felicity!" he called, his voice hoarse with fear.

Dimly, he was aware of the sound of his siblings chasing after him down the embankment, following him through the snow. He sank to his knees at her side when he reached her, not giving a damn about the cold and wet seeping through the knees of his trousers, biting into his shins.

She was alert, though her face was pale. Shock? Pain?

"My lady," he said, cupping her face with his gloved hands. "Are you injured? Tell me where."

"Mr. Winter?" Her brow furrowed. "I… What are you doing here?"

"I heard your cry, and I came to investigate." Impatiently, he released her face, shucking his gloves to run his hands over her person, searching for wounds.

His hands found her stocking-clad calves, skimming to her knees.

"What are you doing, Mr. Winter?" she demanded.

"Indeed, brother. What are you doing?" Gen asked as she reached them. "She is perfectly hale. No need for you to be tossing up the lady's petticoats."

"She has fallen," he bit out. "Your blade flung wide of the tree. She could have been hit."

Gavin and Demon arrived next.

"Speaking of ladies' skirts," Demon said.

"Giving you some competition, it would seem," Gavin added in a whisper that was not a whisper at all. "Let's hope this bird doesn't have an angry husband who challenges him to a duel."

"Shut your gobs," he demanded. "All of you. Except for you, Lady Felicity. Do you have pain anywhere?"

Her eyes were wide, those hazel orbs unexpectedly vibrant with the backdrop of the white snow. Gray, green, and cinnamon blended. He had never seen eyes quite like hers. Why, there were flecks of gold hidden within their depths.

But what the hell ailed him, mooning over her eyes when she could have been struck by Gen's blade?

"The only thing that pains me is my pride," she said, wincing. "I was walking, and then something flew toward me. It sliced through my skirts, but did not strike me. In my haste to escape, I tripped over my hems and fell."

He flipped down her skirts, not wanting his arsehole brothers to see her lovely limbs. And that was when he found the clean cut through the fabric of her gown. One long tear, straight through her petticoats.

Relief washed over him.

"You tripped," he repeated.

She nodded, her tongue darting out to wet that succulent lower lip he wanted to nip with his teeth again so badly, it was a persistent, steady ache. "It appears to be a common occurrence of late."

"You going to help her up or force the poor girl to lie in the snow?" Gen demanded rudely.

In true Genevieve fashion.

Lady Felicity's brow furrowed as she took in Blade's sister. He knew what she was seeing—Gen was an ethereal blonde woman. But she refused to wear a gown and petticoats. She was dressed in trousers, an overcoat, men's boots she'd had commissioned to accommodate her dainty feet, and a man's hat.

"Oh," Lady Felicity said. "Forgive me."

"Thought I was a cove, eh?" Gen grinned. "Don't care for dresses. Never did. They get in the way. Give a pair of trousers a try and see if you do not agree."

His sister held out a hand and Lady Felicity took it. Although Gen was willowy, she was also stronger than some men. She pulled Lady Felicity to her feet with ease, leaving Blade grinding his molars, irritated he had not been the one to act first.

"Thank you," Lady Felicity said, still looking dazed and sounding confused. Her gaze traveled between Blade and Gen.

Christ. Introductions. He was not a nib. Slipped his mind. Fucking polite society, which was not nearly as polite as it pretended. Spare him the theatrics.

"Lady Felicity, this is my sister, Miss Genevieve Winter," he said. "And my brothers, Mr. Gavin Winter and Mr. Demon Winter."

Her dark brows rose subtly as he mentioned Demon's name. "I am so pleased to make your acquaintances."

And then she dipped into a perfect curtsy, sodden, torn skirts and all.

Blade did not know why the sight of her, so elegant and proud even after she had just taken an undignified fall into the snow and narrowly avoided getting stuck by Gen's dagger, affected him so profoundly. But it did. He wanted to…touch her. To draw her to his side. To proudly proclaim her as his.

Or to haul her over his shoulder and carry her off so he could have his wicked way with her.

None of these thoughts were helping, and the cold did nothing to stymie the sudden snugness of his trousers. Now that he knew she was uninjured, his body had deemed itself free to carry on with his rakehell status.

He was barely aware of the murmurings of his siblings offering Lady Felicity equal polite greetings.

"You know Blade," Gen observed, her tone rife with meaning.

Meaning he detected and could not like. Meaning that suggested Lady Felicity knew him. Which she did not. At least, not well enough. Yet.

No. That could never damn well happen. She was not for him, he reminded himself. The trouble was, his cock had never listened to his mind. And his cock almost always won every argument betwixt the two.

Color crept into Lady Felicity's cheeks for the first time. "I scarcely know Mr. Winter at all."

Scarcely?

He clenched his jaw. His tongue had been in her mouth. He had bared her breasts and sucked her nipples. Just yesterday. And yet she claimed to *scarcely* know him. The outrageous set of petticoats.

"Lady Felicity has been making a habit of following me about since I have arrived," he announced then, like a complete and utter arse.

Yes, he was being a churl. He knew it. Could not help himself. The woman drove him to distraction.

What else was he to do?

He had never known another lady like her. And he knew,

66

somehow, instinctively, that he never would again.

Predictably, Lady Felicity's response was instant and outraged. "Following *you* about? If anything, you are the one who has been following me, Mr. Winter. Need I remind you of yesterday in the yellow salon?"

The moment she asked the last question, her color heightened. Her eyes widened. He could read her so easily. She had allowed her emotions to get the best of her, and she had never intended to reveal such details to their audience. Although his siblings knew nothing of what had occurred in the salon the day before, her reaction was as telling as anything.

Still, he could not resist taunting her. Their gazes were locked. "I find my memory rather dull at the moment. Mayhap you should remind me, my lady. What of the yellow salon?"

Her eyes narrowed. She had been caught.

Fuck, he wanted to kiss her.

And bed her.

But he could not do either of those things, not now and not ever. Especially not with his damned siblings looking on as a rapt audience. *Christ*, he would never hear the end of this.

"You were seeking sewing, I believe," she said sweetly. "It is not as if you knew I would be within and invented an excuse to go there. I am sure you go about fetching sewing quite regularly, do you not? Only, there was no sewing in the room in question."

Well fuck him. She could give, Lady Felicity Hughes. She was made of sterner stuff than he had supposed. And it made him admire her—and want her—even more.

"And what if I did lie just to be alone with you, Lady Felicity?" he countered, ignoring the fact his siblings were listening eagerly to his every word. Knowing they would needle him for this later. Not caring.

He wanted to best her. To watch that lovely flush creep over her high, aristocratic cheekbones.

And there it was, as if on cue. Brilliant patches of pink on her pale cheeks. "Did you?"

He leaned nearer. "What would you do if I said yes?"

"Enough of this nonsense," Gen interrupted. "I need to find my dagger. It is my favorite. Please accept my apologies, Lady Felicity. We were having a knife throw, and then one of my arsehole brothers made me lose my aim. I fear it was my knife that sailed past you and tore your gown."

Curse his sister. She had a deplorable sense of timing. Could she not have waited another minute to speak her piece? Better yet, could she and Gavin and Demon not have sodded off so he could speak with Lady Felicity alone for a few moments?

"A…knife throw?" Lady Felicity repeated, her flawless brow furrowed, as if she could not make sense of the words Gen had just spoken.

And aye, Gen could be rough and crude, but she did not rely upon flash as much as Blade and his brothers. In her efforts to open a gaming hell for ladies, she had begun correcting her speech. Her comportment—that was another matter. She was a hellion. She did what she pleased and made no apologies.

Blade admired her.

Not that he would ever admit as much.

Very well. Mayhap, if she asked and he was feeling particularly soft. But no one was pricklier than Gen. The woman was made of armor. Tough as iron. She would never ask. Nor would he feel soft.

Especially with Lady Felicity about, he thought wryly.

Grimly.

What was it about her?

"Dagger throwing is great fun," Gen was explaining to an agog Lady Felicity. "I can teach you, if you would like. Or Blade could. None of us can exceed his skills."

He had better talents he would like to teach Lady Felicity, but Blade wisely kept that bit to himself.

Lady Felicity's gaze went to him, hazel eyes boldly inquiring. "I am certain he possesses a great deal of skills, Miss Winter."

She had no idea.

Gavin elbowed him, barely suppressing a guffaw. Blade elbowed him back, a sharp jab to the side.

"Behave yourselves, you pair of children," Gen chastised.

Gavin rubbed his side and grinned. "We cannot behave."

"Aye," Demon agreed. "We are Winters."

Gen rolled her eyes. "Behave or don't. All I want is to find my bleeding dagger."

"I will help you to find it," Lady Felicity volunteered, punctuating her offer with a shiver.

"You are cold," he observed.

"Landing in the snow has a way of chilling a person," she returned.

"I will escort you back to the house," Demon said.

Over Blade's bloated corpse.

"No," he bit out, perhaps with more force than necessary. "That will not be necessary. You and Gavin help Gen find the blade, and I will escort Lady Felicity."

He by no means trusted his brother. Especially not when it came to women. And Lady Felicity was his. Nay, that was all wrong. She was not his. But he had kissed her, damn it, and he had no wish for Demon and his charm to pick up where Blade had left off.

"I do not require an escort," Lady Felicity protested.

Too bad. He was not allowing her out of his sight. This

cursed female was nothing but trouble. He had known it from the moment he had first spied her rump poking out from beneath his bed.

"I insist," he countered, grim.

To his surprise, no one argued.

Not even Lady Felicity.

FELICITY WAS BEDRAGGLED, wet, and cold. The Duchess of Coventry's suggestion she go for a walk in the south woods had seemed an excellent idea when Felicity began her sojourn. But one flying knife and a run-in with the Winter clan later, she was rethinking the wisdom of her decision.

Now, she had a torn gown, she was soaked to the skin, and shivering.

To say nothing of the fact that she was alone with Blade Winter.

Again.

"You are certain you are unharmed?" he asked softly as they crunched through the snow back toward the stately Abingdon Hall manor house.

His concern for her welfare would have been sweet had he and his siblings not nearly maimed her with their dagger-tossing match.

"My pride is terribly wounded." She cast a glance toward him.

A mistake.

Blade Winter, with a lock of golden hair falling over his brow, surrounded by the brilliance of the snow, was nothing short of glorious masculine perfection. Curse him.

His bright-blue eyes were on her too, studying. "That is all?"

For a wicked moment, she wondered if he would lift up her gown and inspect her limbs again if she claimed an injury elsewhere. But then she quickly banished the notion.

"That is all," she agreed, swallowing down a knot of longing threatening to rise within her.

This man is not for you, Felicity.

Think of Esme and Cassandra.

"How is Miss Wilhelmina finding herself?" he asked, not content to allow the silence to reign between them.

And of course, all the ice she had attempted to resurrect inside herself melted.

She stole another glance in his direction. "She is doing quite well. No recent escapes."

"I trust if she decides to hide herself beneath any other gentleman's bed during the house party, you will notify me."

There was an edge in his voice. A curious one.

She could not resist prodding him. "Why should I notify you, Mr. Winter?"

He stiffened at her side. "I would help you to preserve your reputation, of course."

Her lips twitched. The notion of Blade Winter preserving her reputation was laughable.

"Do I amuse you, my lady?" he asked.

"Yes." She turned her attention back to the path ahead of her, lest she lose her footing in the slippery snow. "I hardly think you suited to save my reputation."

"I am insulted."

She cast another quick glance in his direction to find him holding a hand over his heart. "Need I remind you of what happened in the yellow salon?"

What are you doing, Felicity? Cease mentioning what happened between the two of you yesterday at once.

"How could I forget? Have you given any thought to my

71

question, love?"

His low query sent a new shiver through her that had nothing to do with being chilled and everything to do with Blade Winter. His other, far more tempting question returned to her. *Why not enjoy yourself before you sell your body and soul to save your sisters?*

She had scarcely thought of anything since.

But those feelings were not meant to be. She must not indulge them. Instead, she needed to cleave to her future. Find a proper husband. That was the reason she was present at this house party. For Esme's and Cassandra's sakes.

She tamped down her longing, forced herself to speak with feigned nonchalance. "Of course I have not, Mr. Winter. There is nothing to be enjoyed, and I will only be in danger of ruining my reputation forever by dallying with you."

"Do you know what I think, Lady Felicity? I think you are not so much worried about me ruining your reputation. I can be stealthy. Slip into your chamber better than any thief. No one would know I was ever there. Nay, you are afraid I will ruin you for any gentleman who would come after me."

The mere notion of this fascinating man inside her bedchamber, alone with her, was enough to make her knees weak. He was horridly arrogant. Smug, even. Handsome and tempting and everything she should not want.

Her boot slid in the snow, and he caught her arm, steadying her. Felicity paused, turning toward him. "You are being fanciful, Mr. Winter. You make much of your prowess."

He grinned at her. "Is that what you tell yourself whilst you lie alone in your virginal bed, thinking of me?"

How did he know she had thought of him when she had lain in bed last night? She was flushing quite furiously, she was sure. Giving herself away.

"I do not think of you at all when I am in my bed or

otherwise," she lied. "Indeed, I had completely forgotten your entire existence until you came running to me through the snow today."

Another horrid prevarication.

No one could forget Blade Winter. Especially not after he had kissed her. But the conceited scoundrel did not need to know that.

He lowered his head, his warm breath fluttering over her lips. "You are bluffing, Lady Felicity. The pretty pink on your cheeks tells me so."

The ache within her blossomed and grew. This was foolishness. Dangerous. Reckless. They were halfway across the park, in plain sight of anyone who strolled past a window in the library of Abingdon House. She should not want to kiss him more than she wanted her next breath.

But she did. Of course, she did.

"You wish," she taunted him, aware she should not.

They had reached the place where she should tell him she would continue on to the house herself. That if they were seen, alone—Felicity with a torn and stained gown—her chances at securing herself a husband not just at this house party but ever would be utterly dashed.

Those words would not come. All that did was longing, fierce and intense.

His head dipped a bit more. His lower lip brushed over hers in a fleeting prelude to a kiss. "You are the one who wishes, love."

"Here now, you two, wait for us!" called Miss Winter. "Demon found the dagger."

The moment was effectively shattered. Mr. Winter straightened to his impressive height without giving her a true kiss. Felicity blinked and turned to find his brothers and sister emerging from the woods and starting toward them.

She told herself it was just as well they had been interrupted.

That no good could come of kissing Blade Winter again.

Only a little voice inside her remained.

Why not enjoy yourself before you sell your body and soul to save your sisters?

Why not indeed?

"AND THEN," CHRISTABELLA pronounced, reaching the dramatic pinnacle of her story, "Lady Felicity returned with them all, with a torn dress and looking as if she had taken a tumble. Apparently, they were having a knife-throwing competition, and it went awry."

"You told poor Lady Felicity to go for a walk in the woods, knowing the *other* Winter clan was already there?" Gill asked as he plucked a pin from her hair.

Christabella pursed her lips and considered her handsome husband in the looking glass as he went about dismantling her careful coiffure. The Duke of Coventry occasionally enjoyed playing lady's maid for her, and she had to admit, she loved his long fingers running through her hair. He had a special fondness for her red curls, and Christabella? Well, she had a special fondness for the duke himself.

Still, when her husband put it thus, Christabella could not deny encouraging Lady Felicity to go for a walk where her half siblings had been gathered sounded quite irresponsible of her. However, she'd had good intentions at the time. She most certainly had not intended for Lady Felicity to return, bedraggled and with a slice in her gown. Looking quite as if she had been compromised. Thank heavens none of the rest of the company had been about upon that merry band's return.

She sighed. "First, please cease referring to them as the other Winters. We are *all* Winters, Blade, Genevieve, Gavin, and Demon included. Second, I hardly expected them to be throwing knives about!"

He chuckled. "Do you not know them by now, Belle? I daresay *anything* is possible."

"Well, I most certainly do know that they are all rather…eccentric and unique. Indeed, I shall endeavor to never forget that one must cease all matchmaking efforts when a group of Winters wanders into the woods. Heavens, I suppose it is a miracle they were not shooting pistols instead."

"Or worse."

She shuddered. "I have no wish to imagine worse."

"Making babies cry," Gill suggested, removing the last of the pins from her hair.

"I hardly think so." Christabella frowned at her husband. "Grace said Blade held Lady Gwendolyn as if she were fashioned of porcelain."

"Stealing kittens from children," her husband went on.

"There are neither kittens nor children in residence, aside from babes," she pointed out. "Ashley and Pru's twins are scarcely toddling about."

"Are you certain? I could have sworn I heard a cat meowing the other night." It was Gill's turn to offer a thoughtful frown.

When he was serious, he was more handsome.

Her heart gave a pang. Her shy duke was beloved to her.

"I do not think you heard a meow," she dismissed. "Likely, it was your ears playing tricks upon you."

"Feline meows are quite distinctive, I assure you." Gill drew her to her feet and into his arms then.

Christabella's hands settled upon his chest. Her belly was round and large between them. The babe chose that moment to deliver a sound kick. She gasped.

"What is the matter, Belle?" he demanded, his gaze searching hers. "Are you in pain? Is it the babe?"

"No and yes." She took one of his hands in hers and pressed it to her belly. "Feel him move."

"What if she is a girl?" he teased.

An old joke between them by now.

"You know I change each day in the interest of fairness," she reminded him. "Yesterday was a *she* day. Today is a *he* day."

Her husband chuckled, the look he bestowed upon her one of utter adoration. "You are ridiculous, my love."

The babe moved again, thumping beneath their pressed hands. "Apparently, he agrees with you. But I do not mind."

Gill smiled. "I love your ridiculousness. I love every part of you."

"And I love you too." She wrinkled her nose. "Now do kiss me, if you please."

And he did. Oh, how he did.

Chapter Seven

$\mathcal{M}$AYHAP BLADE WAS suffering from ennui.
Or in need of quim.

It had been a long time since he had last bedded a woman—months, in fact. Lady Penhurst, and that had ended in infamy. He hadn't the time or desire to seek out another. Then, he had been cast away to the monkery.

Yes, the countryside was making him spoony. There were no diversions worth a damn. The legitimate half of the Winter family thought it pleasant to light the yule log and sneak about beneath the mistletoe. The height of their drawing room revelry was games. But after hoodman blind, Blade refused to be lured into playing shoe the wild mare or snapdragon.

He shuddered now to think of it.

And he persuaded himself all those reasons explained why he was following Lady Felicity to the false ruins. His half sister Pru had told him about the ruins that morning at breakfast. She had also mentioned—unintentionally, he was sure—that Lady Felicity had expressed a desire to visit them following her morning meal. Pru had also relayed that the ruins possessed a cozy fire tended to by servants at regular intervals.

Which meant that if he made haste and followed Lady Felicity quickly enough, he could have her alone. Again. And mayhap have the chance to persuade her with a kiss the way he would have done the day before, had not his cursed siblings interrupted him.

Lady Felicity ducked into the ruins, closing the door at her back.

Blade moved faster, his long-legged strides eating up the distance between them with ease. He made certain no one else was behind him on the path—why he cared was curious, because he had never given a damn about propriety before— and then he slipped inside the ruins as well.

She was nowhere to be found in the main hall. Bemused, he tried the first door he came upon.

Success.

Her back had been to him. She stood before the merrily crackling fire in the heart of the small sitting room, hands outstretched for warmth. The false ruins were a fifteen-minute walk from the main house, and in the day's unseasonable winter chill, Blade was cold as well.

She whirled about at the creak of the door, pressing a hand over her heart. "Mr. Winter! Did you follow me here?"

Yes.

"No," he lied, sauntering forward, moving toward her. "Did *you* follow *me* here?"

She blinked. "That hardly makes sense. I was first to arrive."

"I was already here when I heard a door opening and closing." He shrugged, allowing that bit of fiction to settle where it would. "I thought to investigate, and imagine my surprise to find you here."

He was not about to admit to following her, damn it.

Her eyes narrowed. "I most certainly did not follow you, Mr. Winter. Indeed, I am endeavoring to stay far away from you, as proximity has proven quite dangerous."

"Dangerous?" He stopped before her, shedding his gloves,

coat, and hat. He dropped them to the floor. "If by danger-ous, you mean delicious, then I agree, love."

There it was again, that exquisite pink on her cheeks.

A woman innocent enough to flush—now there was a luxury he could not deny himself. She was so damned virginal and sheltered. He wanted to ruin her. To bring her to her knees. To steal a modicum of that innocence for himself. To devour her.

Christ, had he ever wanted a woman more?

The answer was painfully obvious—a decisive no.

"I meant what I said, sir," she insisted, shoulders going back in a defiant pose. "Being near you is dangerous."

"To your virtue? Mayhap." He grinned. "But I promise you that you will not regret it. Not for a moment."

Her lips parted. "Mr. Winter!"

But though she scolded him and pretended she was out-raged, he knew better. He could still hear her sultry moan when he had sucked her nipples. He could have lifted her gown, touched her, and he would have found her wet. He could have stroked her until she spent, and he suspected she knew the truth of it as well as he did. Their connection was undeniable.

"Do not pretend to be scandalized, Lady Felicity. We both know you enjoyed yourself in my arms." He plucked the hat from her head, dropping it to the floor along with his shed outer garments. "We both know you want more."

He was playing with fire, and he knew it. Mayhap they would both get burned. He was not sure he cared at the moment. All he did care about was the hazel-eyed siren watching him with her steady, rapt gaze. Her scent reached him then—jasmine. Sweet and exotic. Like something he could never have.

Something he very much desired.

"You are astoundingly arrogant, Mr. Winter," she accused, but there was no heat in her voice.

He was, and he knew it. With good reason. He may not be a titled lord to the manor born, but he knew how to satisfy a lady.

His eyes dipped to her lips. "Yet you long for me anyway."

"You presume to know what I feel?" she asked softly. "What I want?"

He reached for the line of buttons on her pelisse, removing them one by one from their moorings. "Stop me if I am wrong."

She did not move away. Nor did she do anything to stay his progress. Instead, she remained still, allowing him to undo them.

"What are you doing, Mr. Winter?"

"Time you call me Blade, don't you think, love?" He reached the final button at last and peeled the garment from her shoulders.

He tossed the pelisse to the floor.

Silence reigned for a moment, no sound save the fire popping in the grate. He wondered how much time he had until a servant arrived to tend it. He thought about latching the door.

He would have, mayhap.

But then Lady Felicity did the last thing he expected. She grasped his lapels in both her dainty fists and pulled him closer.

"Blade," she said at last.

And then, she kissed him.

FELICITY HAD LOST control.

Had lost all sense of duty.

Mayhap it was the distance from the main house that had emboldened her. Auntie Agatha would never follow her here—her arthritic knees would not allow the fifteen-minute walk, and nor would her gouty foot. They were alone. No Winter siblings to intrude.

No interruption.

Nothing but Blade Winter, smug and sinfully tempting and so handsome she ached.

She should not have kissed him, and she knew it. But when he responded, kissing her back with so much fervor it stole her breath, she could not summon a hint of regret. As before, Blade Winter's kisses were a revelation. Heat flared within her. She was hot all over, and it had nothing to do with the fire at her back.

She felt alive in a way she never had before, as if all her life, she had been waiting for this man. Which was foolish, of course. She could not pursue anything with him. The gentlemen she needed to be speaking with—her husband prospects—were back at the main house, likely engaged in drawing room games or out riding. If there was any man who was unabashedly not the husbandly sort, it was the man kissing her breath away with such wickedness.

And worst of all, though she knew she should stop, she could not. She did not want to. All she wanted was more.

They kissed and kissed. He sucked her lower lip, licked into her mouth. Her tongue tangled with his. He kissed her as if she were a secret that belonged to him and him alone.

And she wanted to.

Then and there, in the freedom of the false ruins, the hush of winter blanketing the world outside, she wanted to be his. Wanted him to make her his. Wanted him to touch her, take her, do with her as he would.

Anything. Everything.

"Felicity." He said her name as if it were a prayer. Chanted it as he kissed across her jaw. Hot little pecks that left her knees weak. All the way to her ear, where his breath made her shiver. "Sweet, innocent Lady Felicity. What are you doing to me?"

She would have returned the question, asked him what he was doing to her, but the connection between her mind and her tongue had been vanquished by the trajectory of his beautiful mouth. He was kissing behind her ear now, then down her throat, alternating between worshipful caresses with his lips, nips with his teeth, and wicked suction.

Her head fell back. A moan stole from her. She was tingling. Everywhere.

"Tell me to leave you, and I will go," he murmured.

Impossible.

Him leaving was the last thing she wanted, no matter how wrong this was. How dangerous. Auntie Agatha would never discover them here, but someone else could. Other guests, a servant.

She clutched him to her. "Stay."

"That was unwise of you, love. Last chance."

"Do not stop," she ordered him.

And then she claimed his mouth once more.

If she had to marry to save her sisters, before she did so, she was going to do this for herself. She was going to kiss Blade Winter senseless, and she was going to enjoy every moment of it. She would not surrender her innocence. Felicity did not dare to go that far. However, why not seize what was being offered with both hands?

And with her lips?

Their mouths moved together as if they had each been

fashioned for this reckless moment, for this meeting of lips and tongues and teeth. They kissed as if this were the first and the last time. With desperation and awe and an overwhelming sense of urgency.

"Sweet Felicity," he whispered.

She did not feel sweet. She felt…desperate. But anyway, it mattered not. For she could not manage a single response save a throaty sigh. He felt too good. Kissing Blade Winter was forbidden and wonderful. She never wanted to pull her lips from his. Indeed, she was reasonably convinced she could go without her next breath if it meant she could continue keeping their mouths fused.

He ended the kiss as abruptly as she had begun it, tearing his lips from hers and staring down at her. His bright-blue eyes were brilliant and vivid. His breathing was as ragged as Felicity's was. Good, then. He was not unaffected.

But why had he stopped kissing her?

"Blade," she began, only to be silenced by the press of his forefinger to her lips.

"Hush."

"Hush?" she mumbled against his finger.

"Someone is coming," he said.

And that was all she needed to hear for her skin to go cold and her heart to plummet. She pushed away from him, mouth dry. *Good God*, this was how her hopes of securing Esme's and Cassandra's futures ended. Destroyed in the false ruins at a country house party by an East End scoundrel whose most recent accomplishment appeared to be wounding the Earl of Penhurst in a duel.

Because he had bedded the man's wife.

"Remain here," he ordered her, voice low. "I will meet whomever it is. Do not open the door, whatever you do."

She nodded, startled he was thinking of propriety. Of her

reputation. But then again, one could only suppose he had no wish to cause more trouble for his family. His duel with Penhurst was the reason he was in attendance at Mr. Devereaux Winter and Lady Emilia Winter's Christmastide party. At least, that was what Lady Aylesford had relayed. The family thought he could do little damage rusticating in the country.

Her kiss-swollen lips and about-to-be-ruined reputation were proof to the contrary.

More fool, she.

Still, Felicity could do nothing but watch as he turned away from her and stalked across the chamber, quitting the room. Voices echoed in the hall beyond the closed door. Masculine, both of them.

She could only pray it was a servant, arriving to tend the fire. Their words did not carry to her; she was left with nothing save the tone of their voices. Nothing seemed amiss. She pressed a hand to her rapidly beating heart, willing it to calm as her eyes frantically cast about the chamber, looking for a place where she might hide herself lest Mr. Winter find himself unable to keep their unexpected guest from entering the chamber and discovering her within.

There was none. Indeed, there was nothing to be done. She had to remain here, hoping he would play the gentleman, that he would protect her honor. That she had not been so recklessly foolish that she could never recover from this tremendous lapse of reason.

Esme and Cassandra, she reminded herself. How dare she have been selfish? How dare she have given in to temptation?

If she escaped from this folly with her reputation intact, it would serve as a stern lesson to her. She was not infallible. She could not afford to spend further time with Blade Winter, alone or accompanied. The man was dangerous to her reputation and virtue both.

Because he was the most deliciously handsome man she had ever beheld. And because he was also the most fluent kisser. She could well understand Lady Penhurst's defection. Though thoughts of the woman stung—the notion of any other female in Blade Winter's arms did, in truth—Felicity could acknowledge that much.

In what was mayhap a futile action, she retrieved her discarded pelisse and stuffed her arms into the sleeves. Frantically, she began fastening the seemingly endless line of buttons. If she were fully clothed, mayhap she could blunt the scandal's blow…

Oh, who was she fooling? There would be no blunting. The blow of scandal, however it came, was always felling for a lady. And for a lady such as herself, needing to make a match to save her sisters' futures, it would be a societal death knell, pure and simple.

Felicity reached the top of her pelisse, only to realize she had misbuttoned. One mooring remained, but no buttons. The entire affair was off. A glance down her person confirmed she had begun with the second button instead of the first.

"Blast," she muttered, as she began to unfasten them with as much haste as her trembling fingers could muster.

The door opened and her heart fell for the second time.

But only Blade Winter sauntered through. The portal closed behind him. He looked as if he had been kissing someone, she thought to herself. And then she realized he had.

Her.

What a cursed disaster. What had she been thinking?

"Who was it?" she whispered.

"The footman sent to tend the fire," he said smoothly. "I have assured him I will stoke the flame for him. He is returning to the main house now, none the wiser that I am not alone."

Relief fell upon her with so much force, she nearly swooned.

Here was a reprieve, she hoped.

"My lady?" he asked, reaching her, seizing her arms in a grip that was gentle but firm. "You are pale. You are not going to swoon on me, are you?"

She inhaled slowly. "No."

But she swayed. Listed to the left, then the right. Everything swirled. Even his handsome face and his well-kissed mouth. It had only been a servant, she reminded herself. Not anyone who might cause them trouble. Thank the sweet heavens above. It had not been anyone who might have stormed past Mr. Winter, entered the chamber, and saw her there with her misbuttoned pelisse and kiss-swollen lips.

He steadied her, proving the anchor to her storm-tossed ship. "Calm, Lady Felicity. No one shall ever be the wiser that you were here alone with me. The servant is on his way back to the main house."

It could have been worse.

So much worse.

And she had been selfish to conduct herself thus, with him.

So desperately, foolishly, stupidly selfish.

She had not been thinking of her sisters when she had been in Blade Winter's arms. She had only been thinking of herself.

"I must go," she managed to say. "This… I cannot…We cannot… What happened between us was a mistake, Mr. Winter. One I cannot afford to make again. I have far too many people depending upon me to allow myself to make such an egregious error, regardless of how much I may enjoy it in the moment."

Because she *had* enjoyed it, hadn't she? *Oh dear heavens*, how she had.

"What happened between us was not a mistake," he denied softly, releasing her to trail a finger down her cheek. "You kissed me. That was not a mistake."

"Yes," she hissed at him, finally managing to get her pelisse buttoned in the proper order at last. "It was. One which cannot—must not—be repeated."

"Cannot why?" he asked.

"Because it is wrong."

"So you have said." He eyed her calmly. "But you have not spoken a word of why."

"I have already told you." She glared at him, hating herself for wanting him so much. Hating him for being so deuced handsome. The inking of the blade atop his hand mocked her. So, too, his visage. Perfectly masculine. Perfect, in every sense.

Little wonder all the ladies wanted him.

Little wonder Lady Penhurst would forsake her husband.

Curse Lady Penhurst. Felicity wished she had never heard the woman's name. Wished those sweet, hot, knowing lips that had so recently devoured hers had never known another's beneath them.

"Tell me again, then, if you please," he commanded, that brilliant gaze of his traveling over her face, reaching deep inside her to a place she dearly longed to keep from him.

He was getting beneath her skin, this man. He was finding his way to the deepest part of her heart. A heart he had no business invading, a heart she had no intention of inviting him into.

"I must make a match to save my sisters," she said, desperation defeating her pride. "My father has tremendous debts, the sort which cannot be ameliorated with ease or time. I have younger sisters, Esme and Cassandra. They have no dowries to speak of, and yet they must wed. I want them to find husbands who care for them. Husbands who will be gentle and kind and considerate. Husbands who appreciate their intellects, who love them."

He raised a golden brow, studying her closely. "And still, I do not hear a reason why you must make a match."

"My sisters are depending upon me," she snapped. "Have you not been listening? My father spent every guinea he possessed and then he spent more. Without a grand match from me, Esme and Cassandra have no hope."

"And yet, if you make a match to save your sisters, you are the one without hope. Is that not so, my lady?"

His shrewd query cut too close. Because it was true. It was true, and she hated the position in which she now found herself. "This is the necessary way of things. I must marry well to secure their dowries."

She expected Blade Winter to bow and allow her to pass, to let her run from him and the temptation he presented. To make the best choice—nay, the *only* choice—reason allowed. She had a reputation to preserve. All she needed to do was secure herself a husband. It should have been easy enough.

But she had not bargained for the presence of Mr. Blade Winter, or the way he would make her feel.

Aflame.

She banished the thought.

"Why do not they marry well themselves?" he suggested. "Your sisters. Why should you be the sacrifice so they may live happy lives?"

Felicity stared at him, at a loss.

"No quick answer for that one, have you?"

"It is my duty," she snapped, readying herself to sweep past him.

"Ah." He nodded, drawing out the lone syllable in excruciating—and nettling—fashion. "Duty."

She bristled. "And what is wrong with duty, Mr. Winter? I should not imagine you can find shame in it."

"Nay. But I can find shame in a beautiful, passionate lady such as yourself throwing herself on the sword for the sake of her sisters. Let them make matches as they will. Why suffer to make their lives better if it only makes yours worse?"

He thought she was beautiful?

She did her utmost to strike the warmth flooding her away. To tamp it down. To ignore it. But Blade Winter was a force. A force she could neither deny nor resist. And to her dismay, he was making sense.

When he questioned her, she had to wonder herself why all the responsibility fell upon her shoulders.

"I am the eldest of my siblings," she countered.

Yes, there was that. As the oldest daughter, there were expectations in place for her, regardless of her father's mounting gambling debts.

"And?" Mr. Winter asked, shrugging his shoulders. "Dom is the eldest of my siblings, but I never asked him to marry his wife, Lady Adele. Indeed, I argued against it. Thought it would make him miserable. As it happens, I was wrong. I can admit my faults. However, I do not think I am wrong about this. You deserve to find your own happiness. To the devil with anyone else."

If only she could feel the same.

But she could not. She did not have the luxury.

"I love Esme and Cassandra. I want what is best for them, and if I must sacrifice my future for them to gain theirs, then I shall."

"And who will thank you for it?" he asked grimly.

Who indeed?

Still, it did not matter. Every moment she lingered was

one of heightened danger.

She shook her head. "I do not require thanks. The interruption was most fortuitous, and I dare not remain here alone with you a minute longer."

Stricken, she turned away from him and fled.

Blade Winter did not follow, and as she plunged back into the wintry chill, she told herself it was for the best.

"YOU AND YOUR sisters are up to something."

Pru cast a glance in the direction of her handsome husband as they walked through the maze in the gardens of Abingdon Hall. Lord Ashley Rawdon cut a debonair figure, and though they had been married for nearly a year, she still looked at him—her beautiful, golden god—and could not believe he was hers.

"Why would you say such a thing?" she asked, trying not to smile.

"You do not think gentlemen notice when their wives are plotting?" he teased, his voice lighthearted.

"Hmm." She clutched his arm, enjoying the brightness of the sun, reflecting off the snow, the crisp cold of the day. "Mary and Jane are walking now. Can you believe it?"

Their twin daughters had begun their young lives in a foundling hospital, but Pru and Ash had taken them in shortly after they married. The girls were thriving, and Ash was a wonderful father.

"They are determined and brave, much like their mama," Ash told her tenderly.

"Imagine what it shall be like when Edmond is walking too," she said, smiling.

"All three of them." Ash laughed, the sound low and

deep, sending a trill down her spine. "I cannot wait to see it. But do cease your attempts to distract me from my course. You are plotting something, are you not?"

"Plotting is a strong word," she hedged. "I prefer *matchmaking*."

"Between Blade and Lady Felicity?"

"What if we are?"

Ash turned to her and caught her around the waist, pulling her against his lean frame. "You are utter lunatics, every last one of you."

"I am insulted on behalf of my sisters." She twined her arms around his neck, tipping her head back for his kiss.

"How can I soothe your indignation, my love?" He kissed her cheek, then one corner of her lips.

"I have a few ideas," she said, breathless already.

He chuckled again. "I have no doubt you do, sweet."

"You do not think Blade and Lady Felicity would make an excellent match?" she asked as he kissed her throat.

"He is a hardened fellow. Does not seem the sort to marry for love." Ash sucked gently on her tender flesh.

"Mmm," she said. "I think you are wrong about him. He has a good heart. He merely needs the right woman."

And that was why she had made certain to tell him Lady Felicity was going to the false ruins this morning. She and Ash had made some memories there that she would always recall with tender fondness.

"You smell so damned good," Ash told her, rubbing his cheek along her throat. "Do you remember when we had a snowball fight here last year?"

"How could I forget?" She kissed his ear, his cheek. Heavens, she loved this man.

"What do you say we indulge in another?" He worked his way back to her mouth, kissing her deeply. "And then afterward, we can warm ourselves inside."

"Why, Lord Ashley, however do you propose we might warm ourselves?" She fluttered her lashes as she posed the teasing question.

"I have a notion or two."

She pulled his lips back to hers. "Excellent," she said against his mouth.

Chapter Eight

"WHERE HAVE YOU been?" Auntie Agatha demanded the moment Felicity crossed the threshold of her guest chamber.

Felicity pressed a hand to her heart, which was still racing from the combined effects of Blade Winter's kisses, her retreat from the false ruins, and the sheer surprise of her aunt's presence. "I went for a walk."

"Again?" Her aunt swept forward, leaning heavily upon her cane. "You seem to be taking an awfully large number of those for the winter, dear girl. Your cheeks are terribly flushed."

"From the cold, I expect," she said calmly, hoping her lips—which still tingled with the haunting memory of Blade's mouth—were not swollen.

Auntie Agatha's eyes narrowed. "Your hair is mussed, girl."

"I walked into a low-hanging branch," she invented hastily. "It took my hat and got caught in my hair."

"Need I remind you of the reason you are in attendance here?" her aunt asked, thumping her cane on the floor for emphasis.

"I am well aware of why I am here and what I must do," she said quietly, guilt striking her anew over her selfish behavior in the false ruins.

She had been so close to losing everything. She must never allow herself to be alone with Mr. Winter again. He was too tempting. Too handsome. Too opposite of the sort of man she must wed.

He was not noble, not wealthy, and he was a scoundrel.

A rakehell and a rogue.

An assassin, she reminded herself sternly, former or otherwise.

"What will you be wearing to the ball this evening?" Auntie Agatha queried next, tearing Felicity from her madly whirling thoughts.

The ball.

Felicity had forgotten all about it. "I have not chosen the gown yet."

"Then I have arrived just in time. We shall choose it together," her aunt decided. "I have a much better eye for fashion than you do, dearest. It is of the greatest import that we choose a gown that minimizes your hips and does not bare quite so much of your bosom."

Lovely. The prospect of Auntie Agatha choosing her gown for the evening, whilst offering her sharp-tongued commentary, was not exactly thrilling. For a moment, she wondered if she could invent an excuse. But then she resigned herself to her fate.

It was her duty. "Thank you, Auntie Agatha. Your offer of aid is…most kind."

Miss Wilhelmina, who had been sleeping in the bed Felicity had positioned for her by the window so she had a nice slice of sunlight to lie in, chose that moment to rise and stretch. Felicity knelt and distracted herself by scooping up her kitten.

"I have been thinking of which gentlemen you must set your cap for, dearest."

Lovelier still.

She could not help but to think her notion of what a husband should be diverged from her aunt's.

"Lord Chilton is a handsome gentleman," Auntie Agatha said.

Lord Chilton was indeed handsome, but he had dark hair and dark eyes. Nothing at all like the golden good looks of Mr. Winter. Nor did he kiss her maddeningly, drive her to distraction, have an inking of a dagger on his hand…

Cease this at once, Felicity.

She forced a smile. "Lord Chilton is an excellent prospect."

"There is also Lord Wilmore," her aunt went on, "and the Earl of Dunlop is a widower now, looking for a wife to mother his seven daughters."

Seven children?

Good heavens.

If recollection served, Dunlop also had a bald pate and a laugh like a braying donkey.

"He is exceptionally wealthy," Auntie Agatha added.

Felicity tried to summon up some enthusiasm and failed.

There was only one man she wanted to dance with at the ball this evening. One man she longed for. One man who set her aflame.

And she had a feeling he would likely not even attend.

But then, mayhap it was better that way.

A BLOODY *BALL.*

Blade had reconvened with Gen, Gavin, and Demon for a less-dangerous competition than knife throwing. This time, they were playing vingt-et-un in another of the seemingly endless salons the vast Abingdon House possessed.

Blade snorted at Gen, who held the deck of cards in her hand. "There is no way in hell I am attending a ball. Do not tell me you wish to go."

Gen grinned. "And why not? When I open my ladies' gaming den, I am going to have to talk to fine ladies. Lure them in so I can fleece their reticules. That sort of thing."

"Another," Blade ordered her, tapping his cards. "You can't mean to attend a ball wearing breeches and a cravat and shirt."

She dealt him a card, and he was above one-and-twenty. Cursing, he flipped over his hand. "Done in, damn it. You need a gown, Gen. There will be shocked whispers from all the quality Devereaux Winter has invited."

Thus far, she had not attended any of the Christmastide diversions their hostess had planned for them because Gen was, *well*, Gen. Which meant she had an entirely different method of conducting herself. She did what she wanted, when she wanted, as she saw fit. She did not give a damn about polite society, manners, or the expectations of others.

"I have duds," she announced, shocking him. "Pru was kind enough to loan me one of her gowns. We are similar in size, so I think it will do. I had to borrow crabshells from Grace, and they pinch my toes. Can't wear boots with a gown though, can I?"

"Pru is it?" Gavin teased her. "Thought you didn't like the other Winters."

Gen actually flushed. "I need to pretend to be a lady if I want my hell to succeed. Mayhap the Winters ain't all bad. They've been giving me some advice."

"No more cards for me," Gavin said.

"Another for me," Demon announced. "I'm going to trounce you all."

"Smug bastard," Blade muttered.

And the hell of it was—Demon probably *was* going to win. He was the luckiest man Blade knew. He could fall into a pile of dung and emerge smelling of lilies.

Gen considered her hand. "Think I shall stay where I am."

Cards were revealed.

Predictably, Demon crowed. "Vingt-et-un! Give me all your blunt."

Gen and Gavin grumbled.

"That is enough for me." Gen gathered all the cards into a tidy pile. "You were probably gaming us again, Demon."

"Not this time," he claimed. "Nary a card up my sleeve."

That was the thing about Demon—when his luck ran thin, he created his own.

More grumbling ensued, along with some choice epithets from Gen.

But Blade's interest was piqued. "You are truly intending to wear a gown?" he demanded of his sister.

"Aye. And you ought to accompany me," she said, making a sweeping gesture toward Blade, Demon, and Gavin. "I need friendly faces."

Damn. Blade did not dance. He did not attend balls. He detested the frivolity of the nobility. But part of him was wondering what it would be like to dance with Lady Felicity in his arms. To be the sort of gentleman who bowed and twirled her about ballrooms.

"I would sooner give away my entire collection of knives than attend a ball," Blade drawled instead of giving voice to any of the tripe residing in his obviously rotten mind.

Gen's brows rose. "Your knife collection? You *love* your knife collection."

"Aye, I do. Hell, I would sooner scoop out my eyes with

rusty spoons than attempt to *dance*."

He did not know how.

Bastards growing up in the rookeries did not have the luxury of dancing instructors. Cotillions and minuets made him want to punch someone. He would find his half brother's brandy stores and drink himself silly instead. Yes, that certainly seemed an excellent idea.

"Aye," Demon agreed. "But there is a lovely widow in attendance I would not mind spending more time with."

"You do favor widows, don't you, you rascal?" Gen asked.

Demon shrugged. "Mayhap."

Gavin grunted. "Suppose I have to keep you company then. If any of these nibs give you trouble, I'll blacken their eyes."

That left everyone looking at Blade.

"Lady Felicity will be in attendance," Gen said softly, her blue gaze searching his. "Will you have her dancing with all the lords? Thought you would be like Arthur, lifting his leg to piss on every corner of the alley."

Arthur was Gen's hound. And a more ridiculous mutt did not exist in all London. Three-legged and fearsome looking, he was in truth a big, silly mongrel who loved Gen to distraction and would protect her with his life.

"He cannot go and piss on a lady's gown, can he?" Gavin asked, chortling.

Blade tugged at his cravat, which felt as if it were strangling his throat. Could the damned thing be tied any tighter? "I have no claims upon her."

"None." Gen rolled her eyes, her expression blatantly suggesting she did not believe him.

"Just think of her in the arms of all the nibs tonight," Demon added.

Fucking hell.

"I'll go to the goddamn ball," he spat, quite disgusted with himself.

More disgusted with his stupid twat of a mind, which was envisioning Lady Felicity in a ball gown that put her delicious bosom on display, dancing with another man. His jealousy was instant and undisputable.

He had one afternoon to learn how to bloody dance.

HE WAS HERE.

Blade Winter was at the ball. Devastatingly handsome in his evening finery, his cravat knotted with more of a flourish this evening. Golden haired, beautiful. Tall, commanding, dangerous.

Wicked.

He was the one gentleman in attendance with whom she should most keep her distance. Which meant, of course, that he was the only gentleman she could not stop watching. Their gazes had met across the dance floor half a dozen times. And on each occasion, she had felt the connection like a physical jolt.

There was something between them. Something bigger than the both of them.

Something, she admonished herself sternly as she finished dancing with her latest partner—Lord Chilton—and curtseyed to him. Auntie Agatha, for all her faults, was right about the viscount. He was indeed handsome. He was also the heir to his father's earldom. He had been proper and gentlemanly throughout their dance.

But his warm, brown eyes did not make her giddy. His nearness did not cause her heart to flutter. She did not look at his lips and imagine what they would feel like upon hers.

He was, however, pleasant. Polite. He would be the perfect husband, she was certain.

"Thank you for the dance, Lady Felicity," he told her. "Mayhap we should go in search of refreshments. I do think some negus would be just the thing."

"That would be lovely," she agreed, unable to keep herself from glancing toward where Blade had been standing.

He was gone. No longer there, no longer watching. Just as well, she told herself, even as a steadfast ache began in her heart. Blade Winter was not for her. Nor was she for him. She had to sacrifice herself for the sakes of her sisters. She had a duty, and it was not to long for a most unsuitable man.

But then she thought of how easily and tenderly he had handled Miss Wilhelmina. She thought of the way he held her and touched *her*, with such reverence. The way he had urged her to think of herself when no one else ever had.

Before she knew what had happened, she was standing in a room with Lord Chilton. Quite alone. She had been so deep in her thoughts, mind filled with nothing but Blade Winter, that she had been moving without conscious effort. Allowing Chilton to escort her where he would.

They came to a halt. "Lady Felicity, I admire you greatly."

She stared up into his undeniably handsome face, and she wondered if he was saying what he thought he should say or if he truly meant those words. How could he admire her? Aside from dancing together at this house party, they had exchanged precious few words over the years in London. Why, he hardly knew her.

Do not question it, Felicity. You need a husband. Now.

She blinked up at him. "I admire you as well, my lord."

"We are beneath the mistletoe," he pointed out.

She had not known. She glanced up to find a sprig hanging over them, its white berries prominent. She knew why the mistletoe had been placed where it was. Kisses.

But whilst the prospect of kisses from one man in particular filled her with exquisite expectation, the notion of kissing Lord Chilton left her…

Well, chilled.

She was certain that was a pun he would not appreciate. But it was neither here nor there, for in the next moment, he had pulled her near, dipped his head.

"May I kiss you?" he asked.

She wanted to tell him no, but she knew she must not. Mayhap kissing Lord Chilton would prove to her that the way Blade Winter made her feel was nothing special. That the wild emotions swirling through her in the aftermath of every kiss she had shared with Blade were no different than the way any man who was adept at kissing would make her feel.

"I…"

The remainder of her response died beneath Chilton's lips. His kiss was…firm. Warm. Dry. Facile, yet uninspiring. She kissed him back, moving her lips against his in the same fashion she had responded to Blade's mouth. She waited for the frissons of desire to lick up and down her spine. Waited for longing to pool low in her belly. For heat and throbbing to blossom between her thighs as it had whenever she had kissed Blade.

Instead, she felt…

A curious, disappointed nothing. Not one single thing. No emotion, no sensations save a mouth pressed to hers.

Not a hitch in her breath, not a quickening in her heartbeat. She felt strangely unenthused. Almost as if she were removed from her body, watching someone else allow Viscount Chilton to kiss her.

But these were her lips. It was her body.

The kiss ended. Lord Chilton raised his head, looking

down at her with a tender smile that only spurred a twinge of guilt deep within her.

"Lady Felicity, I am an ardent admirer of yours."

She stared up at him, wondering if Blade Winter would ever say ardent or admirer. Undoubtedly, he would not. Instead, he would kiss her breathless and take her to the edge. To the point where she would do anything, forget her duty, her sisters, her future.

Chilton was waiting for her to speak, she realized belatedly. "Thank you, my lord. I am flattered."

And disappointed.

So disappointed.

Because Chilton's kiss had proven to her, beyond a doubt, that there was something special about Blade Winter. Something different.

Something that made her heart pound.

Her knees go weak.

That made her want to swoon.

Lord Chilton extended his arm to her once more. "We have been gone for too long, my lady. I dare not risk anything more than one kiss beneath the mistletoe. I daresay it was enough."

Viscount Chilton was right about that. Their stolen kiss had been enough.

Enough to prove to her there was only one man she wanted to kiss. And it was not Lord Chilton.

Oh dear heavens. What was she to do now?

EVERYTHING WITHIN BLADE cried out the need for his fist to connect with Lord Chilton's face. He had failed to note the moment the dark-haired lord had led Lady Felicity from the ballroom. But he spied the instant they returned. Chilton looked pleased with himself.

The bastard had been alone with her.

Blade's feet were moving, carrying him across the polished parquet. He was a bullet shot from a gun, hurtling toward his intended target. Mindless. Determined to do damage.

He neared the couple, and Lady Felicity's eyes widened as she took him in. Likely, his face suggested he was about to tear off one of Chilton's arms and beat him with it. He wanted to do that. But something stopped him.

An instinct he had not realized he possessed.

It told him he could not settle this matter as he would in the rookery.

And it told him how desperately he wanted this woman. More than he wanted his next breath. Because he was about to be…

Civilized.

He bowed rather than brawling. "Lady Felicity. Lord Chilton."

Though the viscount's gaze narrowed upon Blade, he had no choice but to play the gentleman and bow in response. "Mr. Winter."

Lady Felicity dipped into a perfect curtsy. Her lips had that dark-berry stain that told him she had just been kissed. *Fucking hell.* Instead of the outrage he had expected to feel, the queer sensation overwhelming him was disappointment.

Hurt.

Pain.

What the devil?

"I believe the next dance is mine," he said, as if he had not a care.

As if he were a nib. As if he always invited ladies to dance. As if he had bloody *danced* before. As if he did not want to hang Chilton with his own cravat.

As if he did not also wish to inform Lord Chilton that not only was the next dance with Lady Felicity his, but the woman herself was as well. Which he longed to say, although it was not true. She could never be his. They were too different, their worlds disparate. She needed a husband to fulfill her obligation to her family and sisters. He did not want to marry.

Chilton said something Blade's overburdened mind refused to hear. All that mattered was the lord went away. And he was leading Lady Felicity to the dance floor and Christ help him, but the song was a minuet. He was going to have to prance. And try not to trip either himself or Lady Felicity.

"You know quite well this dance is not yours," she murmured as they took up their positions.

"It is now," he informed her, leaning too near to her ear for propriety's sake and not near enough for his own.

Jasmine, fragrant and lilting, wafted to him.

The dance began in truth, and they faced each other in the fashion of prizefighters squaring off. He felt ridiculous. This was surely the most spoony notion he had ever entertained. They moved, their gazes holding. Strangely, his feet knew what to do. The cursory lessons he had taken returned to him.

What was he doing? Why was he dancing with her? Why were her hazel eyes burning into his? Their hands linked, and they spun nearer each other as the song played on.

"You surprise me," she said softly so their fellow dancers could not overhear.

He surprised himself, but he was not about to admit it.

"Oh?" They spun.

Her warmth and nearness were doing the damnedest things to his ability to think, concentrate, speak. At least his feet continued to move and do as they were meant—

uncivilized clod that he was.

"I did not suppose a ball would appeal to a man like you."

"A man like me?" He frowned.

The steps of the dance separated them once more. He had to wait an entire eternity for their hands to link and for her to hover near enough for private speech again.

"You have claimed to be common," she elaborated. "Baseborn, I believe you said, a scoundrel, a rogue, a rookery thief. An assassin. A bastard. Yet you dance as beautifully as any gentleman."

She was insinuating he was not a gentleman. And she was right. It was a fact he had once prided himself upon. But now? Now…

He was beginning to wonder if he wanted to continue being the man he had always seen himself as. Or if he wanted to be the man who deserved her. The man who could effortlessly dance with her, whisk her away from a ball. A man who bowed and spoke prettily and plied his charm and allowed a valet to knot his cravat into something ridiculously architectural.

"I learned to dance this afternoon," he admitted.

He had attended the ball to see her, for this chance to meet her as an equal. To twirl about a ballroom with her.

They pranced about each other some more, and Blade was reasonably certain he missed a step. Or three. But the smile she gave him made him feel as if he were the best damned dancer in England.

When they linked hands once more, her countenance had turned thoughtful. Her teeth worried her lush lower lip. "Why this afternoon?"

"Because I wanted to dance with you," he admitted. And then nearly kicked himself in the arse.

He sounded like a lovelorn swain.

Which was mad, of course. He was not in love with Lady Felicity Hughes.

Was he?

She smiled, her fingers squeezing his. "You did this for me?"

He was spared from having to respond when they resumed their frolic about each other once more. *Damn it*, he had learned to dance for her. He had come to this bloody ball for her. And she had gone off with Lord Bloody Chilton and allowed the arsehole to *kiss* her.

He should be angry. He should not be dancing a minuet.

And yet, he was. And dancing with Lady Felicity was... Hell, it felt natural. He did not even mind it. Indeed, part of him was enjoying it.

He would have shuddered, or thrown his favorite dagger at the nearest available wall, but he was still doing his utmost to make certain he did not trip over his feet. And Lady Felicity's hazel gaze was warm and unwavering upon him.

At last, the dance came to a halt, and he bowed to her as elegantly as he could muster with the weight of so much upon his chest. *By God*, he could not be going the way of his brothers. Devil and Dom had fallen in love with their wives and were happily married, babes on the way.

Blade had no intention of marrying.

He never had.

And yet...

Nay. He would not contemplate anything else. Not now. Not in the warmth of the ballroom with Lady Felicity's sweet scent rotting his mind. He was still bloody dizzied from all the twirling.

"Shall I escort you to your aunt, my lady?" he asked, pleased with himself for the evenness of his tone.

"Mayhap a turn about the ballroom first?" she suggested

softly.

The aunt in question was leaning upon her cane and glaring in their direction. Of course, he must be the marriage-minded dragon's nightmare incarnate. He was a wicked sinner, and that he knew. The sort of man who did not belong within a stone's throw of the woman at his side.

"Whatever milady wishes," he said easily.

He was accustomed to being alone with her. To being his most naughty, bringing color to her cheeks. This—playing the gentleman—was new and strange.

"Thank you," she told him quietly as they made their promenade along the edge of the revelers, traveling in the opposite direction from her irate auntie.

"Gratitude?" He raised a brow at her. "For what? Showing you what a good kiss feels like so you have the benefit of knowing Lord Chilton's could never compare?"

Damn. He had promised himself he would not refer to the kiss he suspected had occurred. And there went his promise.

The hand on his arm stiffened. "How do you know Lord Chilton kissed me?"

Goddamn it. Now he was going to have to kill Viscount Chilton. At a Christmastide country house party. Quite untidy and awkward, that.

He summoned all the restraint he possessed. "You disappeared from the ballroom, and when you returned, your lips were the color of crushed berries."

That had been rather more poetic than he had intended. It was not as if he made a habit of studying her lips or the varying shades of color they possessed. Nor was it as if he spent any time at all thinking about her mouth…

Who was he attempting to fool? Of course he studied her lips, and of course he thought about her mouth. Every hour of every bloody day.

"I did not like it," she surprised him by confessing. "He was not…"

"Me," Blade finished for her, hoping to hell it was the truth.

The lone word she had been reluctant to utter.

"You," she whispered, so softly he almost missed it.

"Come to me tonight." The invitation left his lips swiftly. Old Blade at work, he was sure. The seducer, the rakehell. The man who took what he wanted and to the devil with anyone and anything else.

He should rescind those words. Call them back. He should not mean them. Should not long for them. He told himself she was an innocent. A bloody virgin. A lady. Their worlds could not collide. He was never going to marry her. All he wanted to do was deflower her.

But was that true? The emotion coursing through him now seemed stronger, brighter, bolder. Different than mere lust.

"Mr. Winter," she said, color blossoming in her cheeks. "You know I cannot do that."

"Why not?" he countered, being his daring self. And stupid. And reckless.

And like there was nothing he wanted more than the woman at his side in his arms, in his bed. He had not learned his lesson, had he?

"You know why not," she returned quietly. "I cannot be ruined. I have a duty to my sisters."

"How shall you be ruined if no one else knows?" He glanced toward her, searching her face. "I am discreet. The business with…"

He had been about to mention Penhurst and the duel as an aberration, but he could see the wisdom of refraining from reminding her of his troubles.

"Lord and Lady Penhurst," she prompted, raising a dark brow.

Hell. She had remembered.

"Aye." He nodded, feeling deuced awkward.

That was also unlike him. He had never spent so much time struggling over his words, trying to communicate. Every other set of petticoats he had wanted had been his, quite easily. But this woman—Lady Felicity—she was not like any of the others who had come before her. He knew that instinctively. Knew it in the same, breastbone-deep way he had known she was trouble that first day, when he had spotted her delectable rump sticking out from beneath his bed.

"I daresay discretion does not lead to duels."

She was not wrong about that. But there had been no need to protect Lady Penhurst. He was not the first man who was not her husband to have warmed her bed, and he knew he was far from the last. Also, he had not cared about Lady Penhurst the way he cared about Lady Felicity.

There it was—the raw, real, terrifying truth.

"I would protect you," he vowed. "I would never allow harm to come to you."

And he meant those words. Meant them with everything he had. And then more.

"Yet you invite me to your chamber," she countered quietly.

He studied her as they completed their circumnavigation of the ballroom. Her cheeks were flushed. Her countenance pensive. She was a woman on the edge. He could sense it.

"And yet you are tempted to accept the invitation," he drawled. "I promise you would not be disappointed."

She glanced up at him, those hazel eyes of hers ringed with long, sooty lashes. She was so damned lovely, he ached just looking at her.

"You are remarkably confident, Mr. Winter," she said wryly.

He flashed her his most charming grin. "I have reason to be. Accept my offer and you shall see for yourself. Or stay in your lonely bed tonight, clinging to your duty. The choice is yours, Lady Felicity."

The gauntlet thrown, he bowed and left her there, standing on the edge of the ballroom.

Chapter Nine

THE HOUR WAS late.

Felicity should be asleep.

The ball had ended well after midnight, and she had danced and done everything she could to distract herself from the last man she ought to be thinking of and longing for. *The most unsuitable man in attendance*, as her aunt had reminded her sternly. Auntie Agatha had been most forbidding in her disapproval of the dance Felicity had shared with Mr. Winter.

If her aunt knew the truth of that dance and the words Felicity had exchanged with him afterward, she would have been more horrified. Indeed, she would have likely packed Felicity into the first carriage she could find and forced her back to London with all the haste she could muster.

She could hardly blame her aunt for the warnings she had issued. They were true. Blade Winter was a man who was dangerous to know. Felicity had told herself, again and again, that she must ignore the sinful invitation he had issued to her after their dance. And yet, she remained where she was, lying in the darkness of her lonely bed, as he had called it, wishing she were brave. Wishing she could seize the chance to know passion before duty claimed her.

Yearning for more of Blade's kisses, touches. For more of *him*, however she could get it.

Here was her chance before she had to wed a proper

gentleman. If only Lord Chilton had inspired a modicum of the feelings Mr. Winter did. But of course, he did not. Was that not the burden of life? Wanting what could never be?

I promise you would not be disappointed, he had said.

Felicity heaved a sigh and flipped to her belly. Mayhap if she would get comfortable, she could surrender to the abyss of sleep and by the time morning dawned, the fires of ardor raging within her would cool.

But when she closed her eyes, his face was all she could see. And the longing inside her intensified to an ache.

Inexplicably, she thought of the conversation she had engaged in earlier at the ball with Mrs. Merrick Hart, née Bea Winter. Mrs. Hart, one of Blade Winter's half sisters, had been telling her about how she had been the one to chase after her husband, in quite unusual fashion. He had been determined to be honorable and to keep her at a distance because of the business relationship he shared with her brother Devereaux Winter.

I faced a moment, Mrs. Hart had said, *where I knew I would forever regret not pursuing my feelings for him.*

It had been a bold risk, and Felicity had told her so, marveling at the confidence Mrs. Hart possessed.

Love is always a risk worth taking, Mrs. Hart had told her simply.

Felicity was not in love with Blade Winter. She could hardly be after knowing him for such a short time, could she? On a frustrated sigh, she rolled to her back once more, glaring up at the ceiling.

Still, sleep was relentless in its refusal to visit her. She was thinking about remorse. About being bold. About opportunities, lost and otherwise. Thinking about the way she felt whenever she was with a certain handsome, impossibly unsuitable gentleman.

What if she did not go to him, and she spent the rest of her life regretting it?

Did she dare?

Felicity threw back the counterpane and slid from her bed.

Yes, she did.

She *had* to.

Before she resigned herself to a life of duty, she could experience passion. Just this once.

MRS. BEATRIX HART, better known to all who loved her as simply Bea, patted her son George's bottom, pacing the length of the chamber. Her feet ached from the ball. And from all the hours she had spent in London just before their arrival in Oxfordshire, aiding in the first birthing she had attended since George's. She had returned to her calling of aiding her mentor, Dr. Nichols, when he had come upon a particularly difficult case. Thankfully, the babe had been delivered in good health and the mother had survived also.

"You look exhausted, darling," said her husband, Merrick Hart, as he moved toward her, still clad in his evening wear from the ball, just as she was. "Beautiful, but exhausted."

"It has been a long fortnight," she admitted, "and our Master George was most displeased I attended a ball this evening. He was giving his nurse his opinion in quite vocal fashion when I went to the nursery."

"Strong-minded like his mama." Merrick reached her and pressed a kiss to her cheek, then another to her lips. "I am so proud of you both."

Her heart surged at his words. Unlike her sisters, Bea had not married a lord. However, what he lacked in lineage, her husband more than made up for in goodness, love, intelligence, and hard work. He ran a number of businesses on his own, and in a year's time, he had built them up mightily.

She smiled at him. "I am proud of you too, my love."

He gave her another kiss, this one lingering, before gazing down at their son, giving his cheek a tender caress. "He is sleeping soundly now that he has had his time with his mama."

Bea dropped a kiss on George's linen cap, love for him so strong, for a moment, she found it difficult to form words. "He needed me."

Merrick gave her a sweet grin. "Just as I needed you. As I still need you."

"I love you," she told him, gratitude rushing over her. She had the life she had always wanted—the man she loved, all his support of her independence, and their babe in her arms. What more could she want?

Nothing.

"And I love you." He dropped a kiss on George's brow. "You were not matchmaking this evening at the ball, were you?"

Bea bit her lip as she considered her answer. The truth was, she and her sisters, along with their sister-in-law Emilia, had decided to aid in matchmaking their illegitimate half siblings—Blade, Demon, Gavin, and Genevieve. Thus far, they had only succeeded with Blade and Lady Felicity Hughes. However, there remained great hope amongst them all for Genevieve and the ne'er-do-well Marquess of Sundenbury.

"Bea?" Merrick prodded. "I saw you speaking with Lady Felicity, and do not doubt for a moment that the men of the family have not taken note of what our women are about."

"I was merely relaying the story of our own unusual courtship to Lady Felicity," she said.

"May I hold him before we take him back to the nursery?" Merrick asked, holding out his arms for their son. "It was an unusual courtship indeed. I do hope you did not mention the bathtub incident."

Their courtship had involved the rest of her family leaving for Oxfordshire without her. She had been alone with Merrick. Deliciously alone.

She cleared her throat and handed the sweetly sleeping George to his doting papa. "Of course I would never mention something so improper. I was reminding Lady Felicity that sometimes a lady must seize what she wants, regardless of the repercussions. If she does not, she will spend the rest of her life wondering what would have happened if she had."

And Bea did not regret a moment of the manner in which she had laid siege to her husband's defenses. She would do it the same again tomorrow, if need be. She could only hope the words she had offered to Lady Felicity this evening mattered to her.

"Lady Felicity and Blade Winter," Merrick said, as if he were considering the match himself.

"They are perfect for each other," Bea said. "We all agree. One but needs to see the manner in which they look at each other to know."

Merrick gave her a tender smile, the one that never failed to land directly in her heart. "And how is it they look at one another, my love?"

"The way you look at me," she said softly. "And the way I look at you. A man and woman in love, who fall more deeply by the day."

"Mmm." He dipped his head and gave her another swift, chaste kiss. "I cannot speak for Lady Felicity and Blade, but I do know I love you more and more each day."

She smiled. "And I do not know about you, Mr. Hart,

but I do believe it is time to return our little George to the nursery so we may get some…*rest*."

"If by *rest*, you are inferring something far more intriguing, I wholeheartedly concur." He winked.

And Bea fell a bit more in love with him in that moment.

BLADE PACED THE length of his chamber, clad in nothing more than a banyan, cursing himself for a fool. Lady Felicity was not going to accept his offer. And yet, he could not sleep. Because whilst the smallest chance remained and there were hours left in the night, he could not settle for slumber. Not until he knew for certain she had made her decision.

He ought to have filched a brandy bottle to keep him company this evening. If he could not have her, at least he could have tamed the wild yearning for her that had seized him relentlessly in its grasp. Giving the bottle a black eye would have gone a long way toward quelling his restlessness.

He was Blade bloody Winter, curse her. Since when did he find himself so enamored with any woman—and an innocent lady, at that—that he had to go chasing after her?

Stupid sod.

He had learned to dance for her.

His hands fisted at his sides as he paced.

Had twirled about and strutted like a goddamn peacock for her.

He ground his molars.

He had dared her to be bold and reckless, had invited her to his bed, and she had denied him.

A knock sounded at his door. So low and quiet, he would not have heard it had he been standing at the opposite end of the chamber. Everything inside him tensed and froze. Three strides and he was at the portal, yanking it open.

The hall outside was dark, but the lights shining from his brace of candles illuminated her beautiful face.

She had come.

Thank the Lord.

Need thundered through him.

Wordlessly, he stepped back, allowing her to gain entrance.

Her hazel eyes clung to his as she crossed the threshold. He closed the door at her back. "Why are you here, Lady Felicity?"

"You know why."

"Say it."

He needed to hear the words. Blade took a step toward her, drawn to her heat. To the desire he saw burning in her gaze.

"I…"

The rest of what she had been about to say trailed off as he reached her. Her full lips were parted. An invitation to sin he would gladly accept. Though she wore a dressing gown that was buttoned to her throat, he had never seen a more seductive sight than Lady Felicity Hughes, barefoot and in his chamber past midnight.

"You," he prompted, running his knuckles along the pale curve of her jaw.

Soft skin. Silken and warm.

"I want to experience passion," she murmured. "I want…you."

He should not have asked. Because when she phrased it thus in her throaty voice, his cockstand was instant. And there was nothing he could do with it at the moment. Torture. That was what this was.

"You want me," he repeated, noting the huskiness in his

own voice.

Her pink tongue darted over her lips, wetting them and making them glisten in the low, amber light. "Yes."

Mayhap not torture. A gift instead. She was giving herself to him. There was no question of it.

He was going to enjoy this gift. Very much indeed.

"Take off your dressing gown."

He wanted to see her in her night rail. *Hell*, he wanted to see her naked, too. But he had restraint. He could go slowly. Part of him feared that if he pushed her too far, she would flee. And now that he had her where he wanted her, he had no wish to lose her.

Though lose her he inevitably would.

Just not yet.

Silently, she watched him, her fingers working on the line of buttons. He would have believed himself dreaming were it not for the pounding of his heart. She was the most breathtakingly lovely woman he had ever beheld. And she was here. In his chamber.

He was going to do everything in his power to make certain she did not regret a second of her decision. To pleasure her completely, fully. To give her everything he could.

"You are sure about this?" he asked, wanting to kick himself in the arse for whatever impulse toward being a gentleman had chosen that moment to rear its stupid head.

She reached the last button on her dressing gown and shrugged it from her shoulders. The fine fabric fell to the floor in a whisper of sound. "Certain."

Hell yes.

He was upon her in an instant, his arms going around her waist and hauling her into his chest. His cock was hard enough to rival a fire poker. The exotic notes of jasmine washed over him. Her hair was unbound, the dark curls falling down her shoulders and back.

For the first time, he found himself at a loss for which part of her to worship first.

He decided upon her mouth. Damn Chilton for kissing her earlier. It was time for Blade to reclaim what was his. He traced a path around her wide, full pout. "These lips are mine tonight. No one else's."

He traced over the seam.

She swallowed. Her lips parted. And then she took him by complete surprise. That pink tongue of hers darted out. She licked the pad of his finger. His knees almost buckled. He felt the sear of that lick in his ballocks.

She had a wicked side, his Lady Felicity.

He wholeheartedly approved.

Blade lowered his head, settling his lips on hers. Gently at first. He kissed the corners of her mouth, her cheek, her jaw, her ear. Her hair was a silken curtain falling over her throat. He grabbed a handful and gently urged her head back, baring her throat for him. And he feasted upon her.

She tasted as sweet as she smelled. He could not get enough. He sucked on her flesh, not hard enough to make a mark, ever mindful of his vow he would keep her reputation from being ruined. No one could know.

"Mr. Winter," she whispered.

"Blade," he corrected, licking the hollow behind her ear until she shivered. "No formality between us. Not tonight."

Not ever, he wanted to say. But that, too, was foolish. Wrong. Tonight was all they could have.

Was it not?

Her hands, which had settled on his shoulders, moved, skimming over his chest. Igniting a fire in their wakes. "Blade."

God, his name on her lips. Uttered in her husky voice. It

was enough to bring a man to his knees. And he would be on his knees for her soon if he had his way. He would be relentless, making her come undone. Licking her until she spent.

"Yes, love."

"If I am to call you Blade tonight," she said, breathless, "then you must call me Felicity."

He nipped her collarbone. "Felicity."

He liked the familiarity of it on his tongue. Liked having her here, in his arms. Wanted more than just tonight.

Impossible warned the voice inside him. One of reason, likely. And yet, it did not feel impossible here in this moment with her. Nothing did.

He traced the second set of buttons keeping him from paradise. The gown suggested the dire straits of her family more than her other wardrobe did. Though it possessed some dainty lace at the wrists and throat, he noticed places where tiny, even stitches had replaced tears. It was well-worn, this nightgown, almost transparent over her luscious breasts.

He treated it with care, though every part of him longed to tear it to oblivion. At long last, the fullness of her bosom, delineated by a creamy swath of skin, was revealed. He caressed her through the thin fabric. Though he had seen this part of her before, he wanted to go slow. To savor this night, these precious hours he could claim.

"Your name is beautiful," he said, mesmerized by every part of her, by the sheer dream of having her in his chamber alone. "As beautiful as you are."

Her nipples were hard buds beneath the linen. He weighed her breasts in his palms and rubbed the peaks with his thumbs until she gasped, arching her back.

Her opened lips were a new invitation.

One he seized. He lowered his head and kissed her. No

matter how many times he had her mouth beneath his, the fire roaring through him was the same. He was out of control, burning for her.

She sighed and her arms wound around his neck. He deepened the kiss, their tongues tangling. That was when he knew he would do anything to have this woman.

And he would do anything to keep her.

Chapter Ten

*H*E KISSED BEAUTIFULLY. Kissed away the memory of another man's lips on hers. Desire was potent and heady, rivaling with the despair that this was all she could ever know. That this one night was all she could ever have with him.

And while he was often so smug and arrogant, flashing her those roguish grins and feeding her those sinful promises, the expression on his handsome countenance when he had opened the door earlier would not leave her mind. He had seemed astounded and awed. The way he touched her, took her in his arms, was reverent.

Beneath his wicked bluster was a man with a tender heart if anyone cared to look and find it, she was sure. Oh, how she wished she could be that woman.

But she could not. She had to marry well for her sisters' sakes. Tonight was all she could have.

Their kisses turned ravenous. Their lips moved in a frenzied rhythm, as if they were each striving to devour the other, to commit these frantic moments to their memories. He caught her lower lip in his teeth, and she did the same to him, nipping at him until he groaned. Their hands coasted over each other's bodies, searching, seeking.

She could feel the hardness of him against her and knew an ache deep within, a longing for that which she should not want. A longing for the mysteries she had read about in *A Tale of Love*. Yes, she had peeked some more at the pages before returning it to Lady Aylesford.

He dragged his lips from hers, kissing along her jaw. "Sweet Felicity. I have wanted you from the moment I saw your arse peeping from beneath my bed."

Her skin went hot at the reminder of their ignominious first meeting. Thank heavens Miss Wilhelmina had not gotten into any further scrapes.

"It is…" She paused, struggling to find her words as he once more worked his magic upon the sensitive cords of her neck with his lips, tongue, and teeth. "It is most indecorous of you to remind me of that…day."

He rubbed the coarseness of his unshaven jaw over her skin, making her knees threaten to buckle. "Have you made my acquaintance, love? There is not one bloody decorous thing about me."

And he was unapologetic about it, too.

Still, he had been incredibly decorous at the ball. Where he had danced with her, and what he had lacked in experience in that minuet, he more than made up for with his innate charm and his easy confidence.

"I like you this way," she admitted softly, for it was the truth. "I like you exactly as you are."

The crudeness of his tongue, the arrogance of his smile, the inking on his hand, the scars of his past, the dangerous aura he exuded, his handsome face. And Lord above, his mouth. Lips like his were in themselves a sin.

His tongue flicked over the hollow at the base of her throat, where her pulse leapt and pounded. "You should not like me, not as I am. Not in any way. You should not be here, love. You know that, do you not?"

"Yes." The admission fell from her lips as she tipped her

head back and clutched his broad shoulders.

"And yet you remain." He gently bit the place where her shoulder and neck joined, as if in warning.

But there was no warning he could issue that would be sterner than her own or Auntie Agatha's. Felicity knew she had taken a great risk in coming to him. That she was taking a greater risk still in remaining. In kissing him. In allowing him to kiss and touch her as he would.

"I do," she agreed.

He tore his mouth from her eager flesh, staring down at her. His bright-blue eyes stole into the deepest recesses of herself. Finding her. Seeing her. "Come with me?"

He released her, laced their fingers together, waiting for her acquiescence.

He hardly needed to ask, but she appreciated that he had. How could he not know she would gladly walk into the fires of Hades if he were leading?

"Yes," was all she said.

He tugged her toward the bed. She went. Easily, her entire body alight. She felt as if she were alive for the first time. As if she had just risen from a deep and dreamless sleep. As if she could do anything, be anyone.

As if she could be his.

They fell to the bed together, Felicity on her back, Blade atop her. Though he took care to keep from crushing her, the sensation of his large, masculine body on hers was a welcome, delicious weight. They were aligned, hip to heart. But the barriers of his banyan and her night rail remained between them.

He rocked against her, the thick ridge of his manhood glancing over the apex of her thighs in the most erotic friction. And even with the fabric keeping them apart, she felt him. Instinctively, she thrust toward him, seeking more. She was wet, aching, hungry. It was as if a knot had been drawn with excruciating tightness within her. There was only one cure for what ailed her.

And it was Blade Winter.

His big hands were on her, sliding the hem of her gown higher. Revealing her knees, her thighs. Cool air kissed her skin. But it mattered not, for she was burning, burning, burning. She had never felt anything like this.

But then, she had never known a man like him.

He kissed her slowly, deeply. His lips moved over hers with so much tenderness, she ached. He rose over her, bracing himself on his forearms, gazing down at her. "Still certain, love?"

He was giving her a chance to change her mind. To flee. And although he claimed to be a scoundrel and villain, here again was evidence he was a good man. Here was the Blade who had rescued her kitten. Who had kissed her breathless. Who had learned to dance for her.

Here was the only man she longed for.

The only man she wanted.

Now and forever.

The realization would have left her stricken for the futility of it, but in the next moment, he kissed her cheek. "Felicity?"

She swallowed against a rush of unwanted emotion, reminding herself of what would inevitably happen after this magical night. "I am certain."

"Thank God for that." He kissed her again.

But just as their tongues tangled, he withdrew. This time, he kissed his way down her body. His lips branded her through her mended night rail, one of the shabbiest garments she owned. But though she knew his sharp eyes would have taken note of the places she had repaired it herself, he said not a word about it. Instead, he worshiped her everywhere, as if she were a goddess clad in silk and gold. He rained kisses over her breasts, her nipples. Down her belly. To the mound between her thighs.

Her hips bucked at the surprise contact. Though a thin layer of fabric kept his lips from her flesh, the heat of him and the way he kissed her there, where she had scarcely dared to touch herself, was nothing short of a miracle. Suddenly, that secret place became the center of her world.

The hem of her night rail slid higher. Baring her thighs. His hands, callused, warm, and knowing, were on her bare flesh now. Caressing, stroking. Stoking flames and soothing at once. Making her wild and weak.

His mouth followed the path, starting with kisses on her knees. Then higher. His mouth dragged along the incredibly sensitive skin of her inner thighs. His hands coaxed, molded, opened her to him. Her legs slid apart. She forgot to be shy. To fret over what he was about to do. The hem of her night rail reached her waist. At his coaxing, she lifted her bottom from the mattress so he could glide the fabric higher still, revealing more of her to him.

There was a voice inside her, the one that cautioned her she must face her duty, that she had responsibilities, the one that warned she was taking far too many risks. But she did not want to hear that voice just now.

That voice could go to the devil for all she cared.

"Fucking hell, Felicity. You are so beautiful." His mouth moved, kissing up her thighs. "I never could have imagined how perfect you are."

She was far from perfect. She had a birthmark on her left hip in the shape of Gibraltar. There was a scar on her right knee from when she had fallen in the gravel path at the gardens of her mother's ancestral home as a child.

Then, there was the reminder Auntie Agatha had never

allowed her to forget.

"My hips are too wide, and my bosom is too large," she said.

He ran his hands along her inner thighs, then grasped the outer curve of each hip. "These hips are lush and womanly. And your breasts are nothing short of goddamn miracles."

He was almost stern as he said the words.

She would have laughed, or mayhap offered a nervous giggle, but his gaze met hers, and she read the sincerity on his handsome face. He meant those words. And he made her feel beautiful in a new way, through his eyes.

Other suitors had praised her face. Written sonnets for her. Fawned over her. They had told her everything they knew they should say. But Blade was not offering her empty flattery. He was giving her honesty.

Her heart went fluttery.

She was falling in love with a man she could never have. A man who was all wrong for her.

"Tell me you know how beautiful you are," he demanded, raining kisses on her center.

She was breathless. His lips on her were nothing short of astounding. Sinful, just like the bawdy book. Heat streaked through her. And then the most delicious bolt of pleasure. His tongue lapped against the most exquisitely sensitive place, sending a shower of sparks through her.

He sucked, then licked. "Tell me you know."

She did not know. Or at least, she had not known, until now. He made her feel beautiful. He made her feel...*everything*.

"I know," she managed to say, just before his tongue glided slickly through her folds, delving deep.

Good she had spoken before he had licked into her, his tongue probing and seeking, because now she was not sure she would ever be capable of another coherent thought. All she could do was lie there beneath the veneration of his mouth, as wave after wave of pleasure crashed over her.

Her body bowed from the bed, seeking. His hands moved over her, caressing her stomach, and she could not look away from the wonder of him between her thighs, his handsome face nestled there, his touch on her. His hands were large, callused, the ink of the dagger there a sharp contrast to her pale skin. She never wanted him to stop.

Duty no longer mattered.

Nothing mattered but this man. This moment.

When one of his hands cupped her breast, tweaking her nipple, at the same moment his tongue plunged deep inside her, she came undone. Bliss slammed into her, starting in her core and rippling throughout.

"That's it, love," he murmured against her throbbing flesh, "spend for me. All over my tongue."

His sinful words only served to heighten the pleasure. She was shameless now, writhing against him to get him nearer. And he remained where he was, giving her what she wanted and then giving her more. Giving her what she did not even know she needed.

His tongue played over her, licking her up as if she were the finest dessert.

"Blade," she gasped, certain she was going to perish from the unprecedented ecstasy.

Her heart was racing at a gallop, her breaths ragged and shallow. Her entire body was humming, aflame, the aftereffects of what he had done to her still coursing through her like warm honey. Slow, sweet, decadent.

But he was not finished. He kissed her there, on her mound, his hands coasting over her hips to cup her bottom and lift her to a new angle. His tongue flitted over the sensitive bundle of flesh hidden in her folds. She was on the edge. So close again.

He sucked hard on the bud of her sex, then slid a finger to her entrance. He teased her there, his finger shallowly thrusting as he had with his tongue. The ache within intensified. She wanted him there, inside her.

"Come again, love," he cajoled. "I want to give you so much pleasure, you cannot think."

He had already succeeded. Her thoughts were a blur of light and brightness, muddled together. She was soaring. Then bursting as another impossible rush of pleasure swept over her. She was falling apart. Shattering into stars. Trembling beneath him. He hummed against her flesh, and she absorbed the primal rumble of his baritone, a new ripple of awareness tremoring through her.

When the last rush subsided, he kissed his way up her body, lingering on her breasts and nipples, before stretching himself at her side. As her wits returned to her, Felicity realized he was still clad in his dressing gown. His lips were dark and glistening.

From her.

His too-long blond hair was rakishly mussed.

He looked deliciously disreputable.

Her heart thumped. *Mine*, it said when their gazes met and held. And she wished it were true.

"Thank you for letting me pleasure you," he told her.

"But you have not taken any pleasure," she protested, confused.

She had thought he intended to make love to her tonight. And she wanted that. She wanted it more now than she had realized.

"I found pleasure enough in making you spend, love," he said. "You are going to be married, and I will not take your innocence. It would not be right."

Could this be? An honorable rogue?

Why?

Did he not know honor was the last thing she had sought in coming here to him tonight? She had taken a great risk to find her way here, to his chamber. And she wanted her reward. She wanted *him*.

"I am not married yet," she said, shivering as a cool draft of air swept over her, reminding her of her nudity. "As you said, no one will know I am ruined."

"I will know," he admitted in a low rasp. "I want to be a gentleman for you, Felicity. You deserve no less."

Her heart gave a pang. "Blade, please."

"You do not know what you're asking of me," he said.

She reached for his hands, feeling brazen and desperate all at once. "Touch me."

"Felicity."

"I am aching for you," she whispered. "If I must spend the rest of my life in a marriage founded in duty, give me this, Blade. Give me this one night in your arms."

"Christ," he bit out, his countenance turning harsh.

He was a man at war with himself, his jaw a hard slash to rival his cheekbones. His eyes were dark and stormy, like the sea at sunset.

She brought his palms to her breasts, rolling to her side so they were face-to-face, chest to chest. "Please."

"There will be no going back, love," he warned, his voice sounding strained.

"Nor do I want there to be." She shifted, bringing their bodies closer. The heavy ridge of his manhood pressed against her belly.

A new kind of heat blazed between her thighs.

A new longing.

"Tell me what to do," she urged when he remained silent, his sole movement in the thumbs that rolled over her nipples in slow, tantalizing circles.

"Damn it," he cursed. "You do not know what you are asking."

"I know, Blade, and I want you. Just you."

Always you.

Those two words came from seemingly nowhere, taking her by surprise. At the last moment, she suppressed them, kept from speaking them aloud. Whatever this was between them, it felt sacred and rare. And she wanted to revel in it, in him, while she could.

Before it was taken from her.

With a growl, he tore open the belt keeping his dressing gown in place. He shrugged the black fabric away and emerged, naked and godlike. He took her breath. But her eyes had only a moment to feast upon his broad chest—where initials had been inked upon his flesh, along with a cross—his taut abdomen, the golden trail of hair leading to his manhood.

He was thick and long and ruddy, and the sight of him both terrified and thrilled her. She knew what he was meant to do with that magnificent part of himself. And how it would fit inside her was a mystery she would soon discover if the intensity in his gaze was any indication.

"Touch me," he said.

She knew then he had made up his mind. He was going to make love to her. To take her innocence. Everything in her sent up a resounding wave of gladness, followed swiftly by renewed desire.

He took her hand and placed it on him there, where he was surprisingly smooth and so warm. He guided her, showing her how to stroke from root to tip. How powerful she felt, touching this man, making him groan. A pearly bead on the end of his manhood enthralled her. She swirled her thumb over it, earning another moan and a thrust of his hips.

With her left hand, she caressed his shoulder, then ran her touch down his well-muscled biceps where she discovered a faded scar. Then on to his chest, tracing over the ink there. All whilst she gripped him, pleasuring him in return.

"Sweet hell, Felicity," he said on a groan, and then he took her mouth.

He kissed her tenderly at first, then with greater abandon. Her lips moved against his, opening for his questing tongue. Abruptly, he ended it, raining a series of kisses down her neck, to her breasts. He kissed and licked and sucked. She continued enjoying free reign over his beautiful body, touching him, stroking him.

They rolled together, Felicity on her back, Blade settled between her thighs.

He buried his face between her breasts, his lips skimming over her, igniting more fire as he went. And then he reached between them, working her bud with his fingers, sending more longing to her core.

"Your cunny is drenched for me, love."

His pronouncement did not cause her any shame. Instead, she was pleased. She basked in the adoration in his voice, the almost drunken expression his countenance had acquired, pleasure threatening to overwhelm him.

"Yes," she said, hips moving, seeking, her hand grasping, stroking.

She was desperate to have him inside her, and she did not care if he knew it.

Abruptly, he took her wrist in a gentle grip and plucked her hand away from him. He lowered his forehead to hers, leveraging himself over her with one arm. "If you keep touching my cock like that, I will spend before I have even been inside you. That is how much I want you."

She kissed him, moving her hips, trying to get him closer to where she needed him most. "I want you inside me."

"Last chance to stop this madness," he whispered into her mouth as he positioned the blunt head of his rod between her thighs.

As he spoke the words, he ran himself over her folds, slicking himself with her wetness.

"No stopping," she said against his lips.

He pressed against her core, where his finger had been. But his cock, as he had called it, was so much larger. Just when she thought she could not withstand another second of waiting, he thrust. He was inside her, stretching her, claiming her.

Pain and pleasure mixed in a heady crescendo.

Blade was atop her, his hard body between her thighs, pinning her to his bed. The intimacy of the moment was almost surreal. She had imagined the act more times than she could count since meeting this man. And yet, nothing had prepared her.

He kissed her again, beginning to move. Slowly. Another shallow pump of his hips. More stretching, a slight burn. It was not uncomfortable as she had been warned it would be by others who whispered behind fans and repeated what their elder sisters, mothers, and aunts had told them.

No, indeed. Everything about making love with him was wondrous. She was more aware of herself than she had ever been, of all the places where their bodies joined in delicious friction.

He guided her legs around his waist and sank all the way to the hilt. The sensation was exquisite. She shook with it. Cried out with it. Having him deep within her felt so perfectly right, so achingly good.

He broke the kiss, staring down at her, his countenance tense, troubled. "How are you, love?"

She cradled his face in her hands. "The best I have ever been."

It was true. There was pain; that could not be denied. But there was also an exhilarating, foreign sense of fulfillment. His concern for her welfare was sweet, though not surprising. She had come to know there was far more to Blade Winter than he admitted and pretended over the duration of this house party.

Here was a side that was just hers.

For now, said the bitter voice within her. A warning.

She cast it aside, brought his mouth back to hers.

He kissed her hard, and then he withdrew, almost leaving her body entirely, only to sink back inside her. Pleasure engulfed her, chasing the pain. In and out he moved, again and again. With each pump of his hips, she thought she would come undone again. But it was not until he bit her lower lip and reached between them to toy with the swollen nub of her sex that the next release rolled over her.

It was different with him inside her like this, even better than before. She was intensely aware of him, so large and thick and rigid, of her sheath tightening on him. Pleasure slammed through her, like the crack of thunder in a summer's storm. Sudden, intense, surprising.

She spent, crying out into his kiss.

He stiffened, moving faster, his every motion heightening her pleasure. On a guttural cry, he withdrew from her. With a low moan, he rocked into the bedclothes between her spread thighs, finding his own release.

He collapsed atop her, his heart pounding to match hers, and Felicity stroked his back, holding him tight.

Never wanting to let him go.

Knowing she would have to all too soon.

Chapter Eleven

*B*LADE HAD NEVER lingered in bed with his lovers.

Bedding them had always been about one purpose: getting the poison out of him. But in the aftermath of making love to Felicity, everything was different. He was different.

Or mayhap he had been different with her all along, and he was only realizing it now. *Hell.* He did not know. All he was certain of was the deep and abiding tenderness rushing through him for her.

Slowly, he returned to bone and sinew—making love to her had initially turned his mind and body into pudding. He rolled to his side, belatedly aware he was likely crushing her with his massive size, all his weight upon her.

An unexpected rush of foreign emotion seized him, clogging his throat for a moment as he drank in the sight of her, naked and flushed beside him. She was so gloriously beautiful. Making love to her still seemed as if it were a dream, despite her presence in his bed.

He never wanted her to leave.

Never wanted the night to end.

He swallowed, caught her hand in his, and raised it to his lips for a kiss. "Thank you."

Her mouth was swollen from his kisses. The flecks of gold in her hazel gaze were more prominent. She had never been lovelier.

"No," she returned softly. "Thank *you*."

"You are the most stunning woman I have ever seen," he told her, and he meant those words. It was not idle flattery. Not his inner rakehell speaking.

There was more he wanted to say, so much more, clambering up his throat. But he could not find the proper words to communicate them. He wanted to tell her how much he appreciated her, how much being her first meant to him.

How much he wanted to be her only.

Hell and damnation.

The color in her cheeks heightened. "You make me feel as if I am."

"Because you are."

It was a travesty that she was not utterly confident. That she did not know how easily she could bring any man to his knees. Including Blade.

A sad smile curved her lips. "I shall treasure this night always. But I should go."

A physical ache sprang from his chest. "Stay with me."

The thick fringe of her lashes swept over her cheeks, shielding her eyes from him. "I fear I have already lingered long enough. The damage to my reputation…"

She was still in his bed, and she was already worrying about the marriage she would need to make with another man. Every part of him railed against the notion.

He squeezed her fingers. "I promised you no one would be the wiser. I will get you back to your chamber without anyone knowing, I swear. Just stay here a bit longer."

Christ, he was pathetic.

But he didn't care.

All he wanted was more Felicity.

She looked as if she were about to argue, so he settled his lips on hers and kissed her. He took his time, showing her all the words he wanted to say, the sentiment, ripe and confusing, within him. He had never been a man given to emotion. *Hell,* any empathy he had possessed had been beaten out of him in his youth. He had fled from his mother's endless string of lovers and saved himself by inflicting further violence upon others.

But this woman—Felicity—the innate goodness and purity of her—humbled him. Made him want to be better. To be a man she deserved. And he was not ready to surrender her yet.

He broke the kiss, pressed his mouth to her cheeks, her jaw, breathing her in. "Stay with me, love."

"Blade." His name was a sigh in her dulcet tones.

The urge to give her a piece of him rose, strong. Undeniable. He kissed her ear, her throat, the delicate curve of her shoulder. "Richard."

"Pardon?"

He dragged his mouth across her collarbone, absorbing the silken warmth of her with his lips. "The name I was born with. It's Richard Barlow, after my mother's maiden name and my mother's father. I became Blade Winter later."

"Richard," she said softly, her hands on him, caressing.

His heart thudded. This was a part of himself he had not shared with anyone. No one had spoken his true name since he had been a lad. "Aye. Richard."

He kissed his way back to her delicate jaw.

Her fingers threaded through his hair. "How did you come to be Blade Winter?"

Her soft query took him by surprise. He kissed her lips again, then raised his head to study her. At this proximity, he found tiny cinnamon and gray flecks in her eyes.

He caressed her cheek. "Blade because I am a dab with daggers and knives. I could win a knife fight blindfolded, with one arm tied behind my back. Hell, I have, and won fifty beans for the trouble. I took on the name Winter after I discovered who my father was, one of my mother's many patrons. And only on account of Blade Winter sounding better than Blade Barlow."

"Oh, Blade. Your mother was…"

"A ladybird," he finished for her. "And my father was a man I've never met. A heartless businessman who left a secret family of bastards scattered all over the East End. I'm not fit to touch a fine lady like you."

And yet he was touching her. Because he could not stop. He ran his knuckles over her cheek.

Felicity pressed her lips to them. "There is no other man I would rather touch me."

He had to swallow against the crashing rush of need her words invoked. He could not find words again, so he sealed their mouths, kissing her slowly, savoring her. Savoring the moment, the connection. This was a new form of intimacy, unprecedented.

When the kiss ended, he was breathless, his cock rigid and ready. But he knew he would not make love to her again. Likely, she was sore after her first time.

"Blade," she whispered, framing his face in her elegant, smooth hands.

The hands of a lady.

She looked up at him as if she were trying to memorize every facet of him. As if she were committing this moment to memory. And he knew the feeling, because he was bloody well doing the same.

"Yes, love?" he rasped, his voice feeling rusty beneath the weight of so much newfound emotion.

"Make love to me again."

Bloody hell.

✳

THE FIRE WAS crackling low in the grate, and Felicity was cocooned in Blade's bedclothes, her body deliciously sore and awakened in new places. She should have returned to her chamber hours ago. Indeed, she ought to be asleep, tucked safely into her bed at the opposite end of Abingdon Hall where no scandal could befall her.

Instead, she was waiting for him to return from the kitchens.

After they had made love a second time—the last more poignant and sweet than the first—she had lain there in his arms, reluctant to go. And her stomach had growled. Apparently, lovemaking had an effect upon not just her head and her heart, but her appetite as well.

She had been mortified, but Blade had chuckled, pressed a kiss to her crown, and declared he would sneak to the kitchens to find them both some sustenance. He was so sweet. The charming part of his nature, she had expected. But he was treating her with a reverence that was steadily chipping away at the wall she had tried to erect around her heart.

The door to the chamber opened, and there he was, bearing a tray and his handsome, roguish grin. The wall was nothing but rubble. Her heart gave a pang.

She had fallen in love with him.

With the most unsuitable man at the house party.

"I managed to scavenge some biscuits and wine," he announced quietly.

Dear heavens. How was she going to be able to leave him and forget about this night? He had left his mark upon her as surely as the ink drawings he wore on his skin. He had told her about his past. Touched her with an admiration that left her in awe. Made love to her in a way she knew no other man ever could.

He had donned trousers and a shirt to descend be-lowstairs, but he rather looked like a golden pirate with his bare feet and his disheveled hair. The buttons of his shirt were undone, revealing a swath of his chest and the initials he had inked upon his flesh.

She summoned a smile. "Perfect."

He laid the tray on the bed and joined her, sitting oppo-site Felicity. "Whatever my lady desires, I shall provide."

His gallant air made her heart give another pang. Each second that passed took her closer to dawn and the inevitable moment when they would part and this would be nothing but a memory. "Thank you for braving the darkened halls and rummaging through the kitchens on my behalf."

"Anything for you, love." He busied himself with pouring the wine.

She reached for a biscuit to distract herself from the tur-bulent thoughts running through her mind. The first bite was buttery and delicious. It appeased her stomach but not her need to think of anything other than their inevitable parting of ways.

"Are the biscuits that dreadful, then?" he asked, his tone turning teasing. "You are frowning at me as if I have given you a raw rasher of bacon."

She accepted the wine he offered to her, their fingers brushing. Heat slid up her arm and settled between her thighs with that lone, innocent touch. "It is not the biscuits that are causing me to frown."

Rather, it was the number of hours in the night, steadily dwindling.

"Tell me something that makes you smile," he suggested lightly.

No one had ever made such a request of her. She thought

for a moment. "Sunshine makes me smile. Flowers, good books, sketching, my sisters Esme and Cassandra, the sound of birds singing in the summer, the seaside, and Miss Wilhelmina."

Also, rakish charmers from the rookeries who kissed like an angel, had a reputation as wicked as the devil's, learned to dance for her, and brought her biscuits and wine at half past three in the morning.

She kept the last to herself, quite wisely. Blade Winter was not the sort of man with whom one fell in love. Especially when one faced a marriage of duty forthwith.

"Sketching," he said, taking a sip from his wine, watching her in that most unnerving fashion he had. "What do you draw?"

"I enjoy sketching portraits," she admitted, "though I am not terribly adept at it. I enjoy the patience it requires, the way it forces me to study a face and grow deeply acquainted with every slash and curve."

A drop of wine lingered on his lower lip, and his tongue caught it. "Have you any sketches here?"

"Of course." She brought her supplies with her wherever she went, lest the urge to create should strike.

And of course, it had. She had been sketching *him*.

"I would love to see them," he said, taking up a biscuit.

Her face went hot, which was perhaps terrifically silly given she had just been as intimate with this man as she could be. He had seen, kissed, touched, and tasted almost every part of her. Somehow, the admission he had been on her mind and heart seemed too much.

"Mayhap." She took another sip of her wine to hide her discomfiture.

"Mayhap?" He raised a brow. "After I have just fetched you biscuits, my lady?"

Her lips twitched as he pressed a hand over his heart as if he had been terrifically wounded. "A lady is entitled to her privacy. I already told you, I am not a skilled artist. I merely dabble."

"Hmm." He cocked his head, eying her consideringly. "Do you know what I think, love?"

There he went again, seeing too much. Knowing too much. Finding his way deeper inside her heart, where he did not belong but was already lodged.

She took an extra-long sip of her wine before answering. "What is it you think?"

He gave her his smug grin, the one that never failed to turn everything inside her molten. "I think you drew a sketch of me, and that is why you are keeping it a secret."

Even her ears went hot. "Of course not."

But her denial was futile, and it sounded less than convincing.

"Why so embarrassed, love? Did you draw me naked?"

"No!" she cried, then clapped a hand over her mouth when she realized she had been far too loud.

He chuckled softly, the sound as smooth as velvet. "If you did, I hope you guessed correctly about certain portions of my anatomy."

"Blade," she chastised, sure she was the color of a ripe hothouse strawberry by now.

He just grinned at her, unrepentant. "Never say you gave me a small—"

"Good heavens," she blurted. "Do try to behave, or I shall call you Richard."

He quirked a lone brow. "That was a heavily guarded secret I entrusted you with, love."

She understood that. The lightness of the moment fled.

"I know, and I thank you for letting me see a part of you

that you do not share with others."

"You are the only one I have ever told my true name," he said, taking her by surprise. "Not even my brothers or sister know I was born Richard."

He was close with his siblings, she knew. The Winters were a deeply bonded clan, both legitimate and illegitimate. One had but to watch them interact with one another to see it.

"It is their initials," she said. "On your chest."

He nodded. "I trust them all with my life, and I would give mine for any of theirs."

"And yet you told *me* your Christian name."

"You gave me yourself," he countered. "Hardly an even exchange, but all this poor East End man torn from the rookeries could offer a lady. Even this repast, meager though it is, was thieved from the kitchens."

Felicity did not know what to say to that. She turned to her wine, only to find she had drunk it all. Was he poor? She hardly knew. He certainly dressed well, and he and his siblings ran one of the most well-known gaming hells in London. The legitimate Winters possessed a vast wealth. But while she knew so much about Blade Winter—how strong and beautiful he was beneath his clothes, how deliciously he kissed, how he felt inside her, how he laughed—so much of him remained a mystery.

And she would never unlock that mystery.

Because he could never be hers.

The fire cracked, reminding her there was a world beyond the two of them. A world she would necessarily return to, within hours. Perhaps even minutes.

"Regrets, love?" he asked, his voice low, gaze probing.

"An ocean of them." She tried to smile, but it was hopeless. Nothing in her felt light or free or happy in this moment.

"But not tonight. I will remember tonight for as long as I live."

He studied her, silent and unsmiling, before nodding at last. "The hour is growing late, Lady Felicity. I should return you to your chamber now. I am afraid we dare not tarry any longer."

She was not sure which hurt the most—that she must leave him or that he called her Lady Felicity once more. Part of her wished he would ask her to stay longer as he had earlier. That he would kiss her again, that he would offer to marry her himself. That somehow, some way, he could be the answer to her problems and the man who owned her heart at the same time.

But he did not ask her to stay.

Nor did he kiss her.

Instead, he rose from the bed, taking the tray with its remnants of biscuits and wine with him.

"I must get dressed," she agreed miserably.

"I will give you some privacy as you do so," he returned.

The perfect gentleman. A veritable stranger once more. The mood had shifted between them, growing heavy and tense.

This night was, indeed, all she would have with him.

He presented her with his back as she slid from his bed, doing her utmost not to shed a tear.

Chapter Twelve

THE DAWN SUN was just rising when Eugie returned from a visit to the nursery. She slipped beneath the covers where her handsome, drowsy husband awaited her.

"Mmm," Cam, Earl of Hertford, mumbled, drawing her body against his and burying his face in her throat. "Where have you been, my love?"

"I was feeding our precious little Julia," she said, kissing the slash of Cam's cheekbone and wrapping her arms around him.

Their tiny daughter was still a source of amazement for Eugie, and although most ladies used wet nurses to feed their babes, she refused to accept the practice. It meant long nights and less sleep than she had been accustomed to before, but she had no regrets when she held their child in her arms. Many nights, Cam joined her, but this evening, she had hated to wake him when she had gone on her evening sojourn.

She was rather relieved she had not, considering what she had witnessed on her return.

"How is our precious cherub?" he asked, pressing a kiss to her neck in the place that never failed to make her shiver with appreciation.

"Sweet as ever." She rubbed her hands slowly up and down her husband's strong back, reveling in his strength and vitality. "Do you know, I do believe there is a bit of wickedness happening at this country house party?"

Cam rolled her to her back and aligned his body with hers. The delicious feeling of him against her chased all thoughts from her mind for a moment.

"There could be more wickedness happening," he growled, giving the bare curve of her shoulder a tender nip.

And to think, he had once been known as the Prince of Proper.

She smiled, love for him rising steady and strong, mingling with desire. "I believe I saw Lady Felicity Hughes and Blade sneaking through the halls."

Cam kissed his way back up to her lips. "Matchmaking your sisters have been up to gone awry?"

"Mayhap," she said. "Mayhap not."

There was every chance that was the reason Lady Felicity had been gadding about with Eugie's half brother, Blade.

She brushed a rakish forelock that had fallen over her husband's forehead aside. "Do you think I should speak with her aunt?"

"That dragon?" Cam gave a mock shudder. "I would not. I do seem to recall a Christmas country house party here at Abingdon Hall where a great deal of sneaking about in darkened corridors occurred."

He was speaking of them, of course. "And look at how excellently that sneaking turned out."

The grin he gave her melted her heart. "I could not agree more, Lady Hertford."

He kissed her. And it was quite some time before either of them had a thing more to say.

BLADE AWOKE TO an empty bed, dazzling light shining in

through the window dressings, and a shocking realization.

He was in love.

He would never, as long as he lived, understand how he woke with that thought on his mind, the declaration written on his heart. But he had. And it was true. Shockingly, utterly mad. And true. The unrelenting knowledge that last night had changed everything—that mayhap, even, everything had changed the moment he had first stared into Felicity's hazel eyes—could not be denied.

"Spoony prick," he muttered.

Aye, that was what he was. A spoony, stupid arsehole. What had he been thinking, inviting an innocent lady to his chamber? What had he expected would come of such lunacy? Holding her afterward, talking all night long. Fetching her biscuits from the kitchens as if he were her fucking footman.

And then to wake this morning, realizing the unthinkable had happened and Blade Winter had fallen in love—with a *lady* at that? *Hell*, it was too much. *He* was too much.

Escorting her to her chamber in the early hours of the morning through the shadows had been pure and utter torture. But he had told himself he must be firm. That the lady had made herself clear—she needed to marry a wealthy lord, and while Blade had plenty of blunt, he would never be an earl or a bloody duke.

His mind hurt. He tried to turn it to something else. Anything else. Frantically, his eyes scoured the chamber for any signs Felicity had indeed spent hours in his chamber with him the night before. That he had not dreamed the entire affair. There was nary a hint of her, save the scent of her on his bedclothes. Seductive woman and jasmine.

His cockstand was instant and aching. None of these realizations were helping matters one whit.

Belatedly, it occurred to him that there could only be one

source for the unusual morning light radiating from behind the curtains.

Freshly fallen snow.

He rose from the bed, drawn to that brightness. Naked as a babe, he crossed the room and drew back the window dressings. Below, and as far as the eye could see, spread a hoary blanket, interrupted only by trees in the distance.

It quite took his breath, that dreamy winter's vision.

There was something ridiculously pristine about snow in Oxfordshire. Neat, glistening, perfectly white, and not besmirched by passing carts, carriages, hacks, horse dung, rat shit, donkey piss, chamber pots, and whatever other misery could be visited upon purity. He had never stopped to admire snow in the rookery. Even after first fall, it was gray with soot, trampled by hooves and boots, soiled and ugly and cold.

But this morning, he noticed the snow. He saw its beauty, its rarity.

Not unlike Lady Felicity Hughes.

She was rare and pristine and beautiful in a way he had never appreciated a woman. Hell, in a way he had never known. Until he had besmirched her, just like rookery snow.

Damnation. What was he going to do?

A sudden flurry of motion came into view below.

He recognized the laughing forms of his half siblings, Demon, Gavin, and Genevieve. They were having the devil's own time at this house party. Romping in the snow. Laughing. Gen had even worn a gown and attended a ball. It was bloody unheard of. And what had he done? He had fallen in love and despoiled an innocent.

Dom and Devil were going to hand him his arse.

He was meant to have stayed out of trouble. Instead, he had found more trouble than he had left in London. Only, this was the sort of trouble he wanted to claim. He inhaled slowly, then exhaled, lowering his forehead to the cold pane with more force than he had intended.

His head connected with a thump. He winced.

Hell, mayhap he deserved that blow. Mayhap it would force some sense into him. Nay, he was still stupidly in love with a lady he could never have beyond what they had shared last night.

Belatedly, he realized his siblings had spied him. They were saying something, gesturing, laughing harder. But he could not make out their words.

Had Gavin just told him he could *breathe a trick*?

That made no bloody sense.

He made a rude gesture down at the trio. Demon tossed a snowball in his direction. It landed on the glass with a thud, a ball of white clinging to the pane.

More laughter from below.

He can seal your brick, Demon was shouting now.

Losing his patience, Blade opened the window at last, thrusting his head out against a blast of crisp, frigid air.

"Eh?" he called back. "What is it, you lot of criminals?"

"We can see your prick!" shouted Gavin.

Well, good Christ and all that was holy. He glanced down. The window was longer than he had realized. And there he stood, bare-arsed for all the monkery to see. Or in this instance, for his despicable siblings, whom he loved despite their glee at his abject humiliation.

He shielded himself with two hands.

"Stupid sod," Demon added for good measure, laughing uproariously.

Gen clapped a gloved hand over her eyes. "Can't see nothing."

At least one of them had some fucking manners.

"Not that I expect I could," she added, laying ruin to that

naïve thought in the next breath. "Too small to see from here!"

He slammed the window closed, the laughter of his siblings ringing in his ears, and thrust the window dressings closed.

"Well," he muttered to himself. "That was one hell of a way to begin the day."

Realizing he was in love, then inadvertently putting his cock on display.

Curse it all.

His insufferable siblings were going to bloody well have to help him with this hopeless muddle. But first, he needed to get dressed.

SEVERAL HOURS LATER, Blade waited for the raucous peals of laughter to quiet.

"And there he was, standing in the window," Demon was regaling the rest of their siblings in the yellow salon.

Blade stared at the pastoral landscapes dotting the walls and the winter's sunshine filtering into the chamber's westward-facing windows, fists clenched at his sides, doing his utmost to avoid planting his brother a facer. Following breakfast—where Felicity had been conspicuously absent—he had asked his entire family, Winters born on both sides of the blanket, to join him in the yellow salon. But before he had been able to request the aid of his siblings, the trio who had witnessed his window incident earlier had decided to entertain everyone with the tale.

"Naked as the day he was born," Gen added, laughing her traitorous head off.

He would get even with her for this, he vowed. He'd

sprinkle pepper on her hair whilst she was sleeping. Or let a mouse loose in her chamber.

Gavin wiped a tear of hilarity from his cheek and joined in the familial banter. "Fortunately, he has such a small—"

"What an amusing story," Lady Emilia interrupted brightly before Gavin could complete his sentence. "Thank you for sharing it with us!"

Blade remained unruffled by the last bit. Nothing about his cock was small, and he damn well knew it.

"Quite amusing to discover you have been parading about in the nude before my houseguests," Devereaux said coolly. "I do recall warning you to stay out of trouble."

Yes, his half brother had. And Blade would have reminded Devereaux that he was indeed staying out of trouble—*hell*, he had even danced a goddamn minuet at a stupid ball like some spoony nib twat—except he could hardly claim innocence after last night.

"I was hardly parading," he said with practiced calm. "I was standing perfectly still. And it was unintentional. I have been taking your words of caution to heart."

Except for the part where he had bedded a virginal lady—twice—the night before.

But he would not apologize for that. Especially not when he was about to make amends. Or to do his damnedest to try, anyway.

"Hmm," was all his half brother said.

"Why have you called us here, Blade?" Gen asked. "Surely it was not so we could humiliate you before the other Winters."

"There is no more other Winters," Devereaux said. "We have had our great pax. No more fighting between us, no division between siblings. We are all Winters."

Gen's eyes narrowed, her natural cynicism on display. "I

still don't understand how a man who wants to be a nib benefits from bringing his bastard siblings born in the rookeries to a house party filled with other nibs."

Damn it, his troublesome sister and her outspoken nature ordinarily did not bother him one whit, but in this instance, he did not want the subject to divert from his intention.

"Because we stand stronger together than we can divided," Devereaux countered.

"Strange way for a cove to think, all I'm saying," Gen offered with a shrug.

"We love you," Lady Emilia added. "We have weathered the storm of polite society in the past, and we shall do so again, however we must."

"The most important thing is that we are family," Mrs. Merrick Hart said.

"All of us," the Countess of Hertford agreed.

"No other reward necessary," said Lady Aylesford. "Except, mayhap the story about Blade at the window. That was quite rewarding."

Everyone laughed. Even Lady Emilia, who had stopped the initial discussion.

Fucking hell.

Blade's face was aflame, which was ridiculous. Blade Winter did not flush, not with embarrassment, or otherwise.

"We love you," Lady Pru Rawdon said after everyone's chuckles had abated.

"And we are doing everything in our power to see you wed to Lady Felicity Hughes," the Duchess of Coventry announced.

"Christabella!" A chorus of scandalized chastisements rose up from all the females in the chamber.

Save Gen, that was. She was still glowering at the chamber and suspecting everyone of a secret plot.

"He may as well know," the duchess argued. "Else we shall be here all day, and I am getting quite hungry."

"You just had breakfast," grumbled Lady Aylesford.

"Grace!" snapped Pru. "Next you shall resort to pulling hair."

Lady Aylesford rolled her eyes. "I have not pulled anyone's hair in years, and you know it, reluctant though you may be to allow me to forget the actions I made when a child."

Hell and damnation. The family meeting he had called was descending into chaos.

He cleared his throat loudly and made his announcement. "I want to marry Lady Felicity Hughes, and I need your help."

FELICITY WAS MISERABLE.

She lay on her side in bed beneath the counterpane, Miss Wilhelmina against her, sleeping sweetly, her little tail curled around her body. She had not been able to sleep since Blade had escorted her to her chamber door. They had gone undetected, thank heavens. Her reputation was intact, as he had promised.

Her heart, however, was not.

It had been dashed to bits as she laid in the darkness, only her kitten's comforting warmth and needy purrs to keep her from swirling deeper into the waters of despair. When Auntie Agatha had arrived at her chamber after eight o'clock, inquiring as to breakfast, Felicity had declined, claiming to have her courses.

Auntie Agatha had not argued. Instead, she had seen a tray of kippers and eggs sent to Felicity, which had done nothing other than make Felicity's stomach churn. She could not abide by kippers, though her aunt swore eating them for breakfast was restorative, particularly at a certain monthly time.

Felicity had not eaten a bite. She had sent the tray away, untouched.

She did not know how she was expected to carry on, smiling and flirting, dancing and being led beneath the mistletoe, playing snapdragon and taking sleigh rides, when all she wanted was more of what she had experienced last night.

Her heart knew she could not have Blade Winter. Heavens, he had not spoken one tender sentiment to her. Had not Auntie Agatha warned her about him? Rakehells seduced and charmed, and then they disappeared into the darkness when the pleasure was over, just as Blade had.

She told herself she ought not be heartbroken over him.

But her heart had ideas of its own, and it was refusing to concede.

She sighed, giving Miss Wilhelmina's head a scratch. "It is not fair, is it, darling? Why did he have to be so sweet and charming?"

And why had he confessed his Christian name to her?

Unless he had been lying, and they were the same words he gave all his conquests.

No. The moment the question entered her mind, she banished it, for nothing she knew of Blade suggested he was a dishonest man.

A sudden knock at her door interrupted her miserable thoughts.

"Who is it?" she asked, hoping it was not Auntie Agatha bearing a tray of cockles and anchovy next.

"It is a great number of Winter ladies," called the crisp, patrician accents of her hostess, Lady Emilia Winter.

"Speak for yourself," another voice said. "I ain't no lady."

The latter was undeniably Miss Genevieve Winter.

Felicity sat up and hastily removed herself from the bed. Miss Wilhelmina rose and stretched, then yawned. She glanced down at her gown to find it hopelessly wrinkled from the time she had spent sulking beneath the bedclothes.

Drat.

She was going to have to see all the Winter ladies looking as if she had been hiding in her chamber after being ruined the night before. Which was exactly what had happened.

She cast a quick glance at herself in the cheval, smoothed her skirts and hair as best she could, and then opened the door. The faces of seven Winter ladies stared back at her.

Lady Emilia was at the forefront, smiling in that kind, genuine way of hers. "Lady Felicity, may we come in?"

"Of course." What choice did she have?

More importantly, what did her unexpected guests want?

One by one, they entered, Genevieve last, clad in breeches and coat. Felicity closed the door at their backs, then turned to face them all. For a moment, she feared she had been discovered, that someone had seen her and Blade sneaking through the halls in the early hours of the morning.

Her heart thumped with dread.

"Likely you are wondering at the somewhat unprecedented presence of us all in your chamber, Lady Felicity," Lady Emilia said.

Felicity blinked. "If you are here to convince me to play more games, I fear I am not feeling spirited enough."

"Games are all excellent fun," Lady Prudence agreed sagely. "However, that is not the reason we are here."

"Not all games are excellent fun," Genevieve grumbled. "Nothing compares to a knife-throwing competition."

Felicity gave Blade's half sister a weak smile, recalling all too well the results, albeit unintended, of the knife-throwing competition she had inadvertently stumbled upon. "Indeed."

"Never mind knife throwing," Lady Aylesford said with a dismissive wave of her hand. "We came to talk to you about your sisters."

"Esme and Cassandra? What of them?"

"We understand your sisters are in need of some match-making expertise," Mrs. Hart added.

"And no one is better at matchmaking than Emilia," Lady Hertford said.

"We are all proof," the Duchess of Coventry offered with a bright smile. "Well, except Bea. But she was always in love with Mr. Hart, and their marriage was quite inevitable. The rest of us found our husbands at last year's country house party."

"I am not alone responsible for the matches, of course," Emilia told her. "My sisters-in-law are all lovely and kind, and they stole their husbands' hearts with ease. However, I propose my sponsorship for both your sisters when they make their debuts. I would be more than happy to take them under my wing and see them happily settled."

"It would be one less worry for you," Genevieve pointed out. "Two, actually."

"That is kind of you." The offer was indeed generous. "However, I am afraid seeing my sisters wed is not the main problem facing me. My father has… His gambling debts are tremendous. I must make a good match myself to give Esme and Cassandra the seasons they deserve."

"I would not just facilitate matchmaking for your sisters," Emilia told her gently. "I would for you as well, if you will allow it."

The thought of making a match with anyone made her ill. "Thank you, Lady Emilia, but I am afraid I haven't the luxury of time. I must find a husband before Christmas and wed him as soon as possible."

"There are many eligible gentlemen in attendance," Lady Prudence said.

"Dozens," Mrs. Hart agreed.

"Have you anyone in mind?" the Duchess of Coventry asked.

Blade's face came to mind, and her foolish, weak heart would not cease its futile yearning for him. That was hopeless, and she knew it.

"Have you, Lady Felicity?" prodded Lady Aylesford.

For a moment, she imagined unburdening herself completely to the group of women assembled before her. But she did not dare entrust her secret. If anyone discovered she had been in Blade's chamber last night, in his bed, she would be disastrously ruined. A lifetime as a companion or a governess awaited her.

"No," she managed at last. "There is no one I have in mind."

"That is excellent," Lady Emilia pronounced.

Felicity frowned. "It is?"

"Yes." Her hostess beamed back at her. "I have already arranged for the perfect gentleman to meet you beneath the mistletoe in the library in half an hour's time."

Her heart plummeted to the soles of her slippers. "I am afraid I cannot. My Auntie Agatha would disapprove wholeheartedly."

"Leave her to us," Lady Aylesford said.

"My reputation," she tried next. "I do not dare jeopardize it in such reckless fashion."

"Nonsense." Mrs. Hart made a dismissive gesture, as if she were chasing a fly. "We will make certain your reputation remains intact."

She swallowed down a knot of uncertainty. How could

she persuade this determined group of seven ladies that she had no wish to meet a gentleman beneath the mistletoe when she was hopelessly in love with another man? Her heart needed time to grieve.

"I cannot," she said weakly.

"Wrong answer," Genevieve said, grinning. "You can, and you will."

Chapter Thirteen

*B*LADE PACED THE library for what must have been the hundredth time. He had been awaiting Felicity for a small eternity, practicing in his mind everything he would say. Planning all his methods of persuasion. Praying his eccentric family would not ruin his chances at convincing her to marry him.

He raked his fingers through his hair as he turned on his heel and commenced a new row of pacing. *Hell*, before this was through, he was going to have worn a hole through the damned Aubusson. Mayhap he would have no hair left on his head either, having pulled it all out.

Where the devil was she?

Why had she not arrived?

The mistletoe hung low from the rafters of the second level of the library mocked him, its white berries waiting to be plucked. Felicity was supposed to meet him there.

She *had* to meet him there.

The door to the library opened.

She stood on the threshold, her expression pained, until her gaze settled upon him. He was moving toward her before he even comprehended it, drawn to her as ever. She was his, damn it. He just had to make her see the rightness of them being together.

"Felicity." He stopped before her, reminding himself he

needed to act the gentleman.

He bowed.

"Blade?" Her brow was furrowed. "What are you doing here?"

Christ. That was not the reaction he had been hoping for. He straightened. "Waiting for you."

"You are the perfect gentleman?" she asked, lips parting.

He wanted to kiss her senseless. To toss her over his shoulder and carry her away from everyone and everything.

"I'm neither a gentleman nor perfect," he answered, flashing her a grin, the one he knew showed his dimple. "But I am the man who loves you."

Her hazel eyes went wide. "You...what?"

"I love you, Felicity." It was deuced difficult to make his confession past the knot rising in his throat, but he managed the words.

Had to. No choice. This was not a game of vingt-et-un. This was the rest of his life. If he wanted to win the lady, there was no bluffing.

"You love me?"

She looked as if she were about to call for her smelling salts.

"I think I fell in love with you the moment I saw your arse." His grin deepened.

"Blade," she chastised, her cheeks turning that utterly charming shade of pink he adored.

Adored?

Hell, yes.

It was a word he never would have used before. But it was a word that went quite well with the way he felt about the woman before him. The woman who mothered a lost kitten and planned to sacrifice her future for the sisters she loved. The woman who was bold and brave, who looked past his faults and saw him as a man instead of a lowborn bastard from the rookeries.

The woman he wanted to make his wife.

"What?" he teased her with feigned innocence. "I was referring to the day you were poking about beneath my bed, trying to rescue your kitten. Not last night."

Predictably—and deliciously—her color heightened. "You did not see my bottom last night."

"Oh yes, love, I did. And I assure you, it was as beautiful as the rest of you."

Also true. Moreover, he could not bloody wait to see it again.

"Do you truly love me?" she blurted next.

Ah, now they were back to the proper subject. "Yes. I truly love you."

Belatedly, it occurred to him that she had not made any declaration of her own feelings. That it was entirely possible he was alone in the way he felt. That she did not love him back.

He told himself he would make the best of whatever situation he was presented with. If she did not love him now, perhaps she could grow to love him in time. He could love her enough for the both of them, he was certain.

"Oh, Blade." She bit her lip, her hazel eyes glistening. "I love you too."

Thank fuck for that. It would have been bloody awful if she hadn't. No denying it.

Blade would have hauled her into his arms and kissed her until they were both breathless, but then he recalled they were not in their proper place just yet. He intended to get this business right.

He held his hand out for her. "Come with me."

She settled her hand in his without hesitation, their fingers entwining. "Where are you taking me?"

"Not far," he promised.

Only to the mistletoe. Not that he required an excuse to kiss her. But everything about this moment felt sacred. He did not want to ask her to marry him by the door.

She went with him. "Loving each other changes nothing. I still have to marry well for the sakes of my sisters, and you have no wish to wed. Do you?"

He stopped them beneath the mistletoe and took both her hands in his. "Marry me."

"Marry you?"

Damnation, he had meant to say something flowery and sweet. Something about how he was not a gentleman, but he would do everything in his power to become the husband she deserved and no less. He had not even asked her. Rather, he had issued the words as a demand. If he could, he would have kicked his own arse. He had no excuse save the anxiousness swirling within him, along with the fear of her refusal.

His hands trembled. Quite embarrassing, that.

He took a deep breath and tried again. "What I meant to say was I ain't a gentleman. No secret there. You won't be marrying well if you marry me. But you will be marrying a man who loves you. A man who will do everything to try to make himself worthy of you. I may be from the East End and born on the wrong side of the blanket, but…"

She held a finger to his lips. "Stop. Stop talking. You want to marry me?"

He nodded, because her finger was still in place. He kissed the pad. "Yes."

"And you love me?"

"Stupidly. I'm a spoony son of a—"

She pulled his head to hers and replaced her finger with her mouth. He had hardly finished his entire declaration, but there was only one thing to do when his woman kissed him, and that was kiss her back.

Thoroughly.

When it ended, they were both breathless. She cupped his face. "Do you truly want to marry me?"

"Trust me, love, marriage is not the sort of thing a man jests about," he told her, trying for some levity before he humiliated himself by falling to his knees and begging her to accept his offer. "I want to make you my wife. I know I am not a lord, but I also ain't a pauper. I have enough blunt to give your sisters dowries. Dom and Devil have moved to Mayfair, and I will find a house there too. Lady Emilia has offered to take your sisters under her wing and help with their seasons. I'll help your father with his debts—"

Her finger returned, pressing to his lips.

"Hush," she ordered him. "You do not have to do any of those things for me."

"I know I do not have to," he countered against her finger, his words slightly muffled. "I want to, Felicity."

"My father will not approve, and neither will my Auntie Agatha," she said, worrying her lower lip.

Exquisite torture, watching that.

"You have reached your majority. We do not need approval. And my family has promised they will do their utmost to aid us however we require it."

"I do not have a dowry to speak of either. What little I had, my father has lost."

"I don't need a dowry." He kissed her finger once more. "All I want is you."

"Is it true what you said to me before?" she asked softly, removing her finger so he could speak uninhibited. "That you keep your family interests safe by inflicting pain upon others?"

Here was his past, coming back to haunt him. Before he

had found his way to Devil and Dom and the three of them had formed a united team—long before Gavin, Gen, and Demon had found their way into the bastard Winter familial fold, Blade had killed in exchange for money. He had been a youth, earning his keep on the streets.

It was a part of his past he could never change, regardless of how deep his regrets.

A part which had served him well in the East End Winter empire.

"I have been seeing to the protection of my family's interests, however I must." He paused, searching for the words. "I have committed a great many sins. I am not a good man, and I will not pretend I deserve you. I cannot change what I have done or who I am. But now, I want… I want to be something more."

He had no plan as to what that something was. But he was beginning to think he might have a head for business. That he did not need to merely be the brawn.

"You are wrong, Blade," she said, her gaze searching his. "You *are* a good man, and you *do* deserve me. We deserve each other."

She was the one who was wrong, but by God, he was not going to argue the matter.

He caressed her cheek. "Does this mean you will be my wife?"

"Yes." She smiled up at him, lovely and radiant and his, damn it. "As long as you promise to never again call me Lady Francine."

He grinned, thinking of their first meeting. "I was only teasing you then, love."

"And to cease referring to Miss Wilhelmina as Miss Whistlewhiskers," she added.

Hell.

He kissed her nose. "I promise to remember the feline's name. Have you any other rules I must know?"

"One more," said his future wife.

He raised a brow, waiting.

"Kiss me," she ordered him, grinning.

"With pleasure." His head dipped and he took her mouth with his, there beneath the mistletoe.

Yes, he was collecting each one of those bloody berries for his own before he was done. One for every kiss.

And then some.

"I REFUSE TO believe it." Auntie Agatha threw her hand to her brow. "Where is my hartshorn? I fear I shall have need of it again."

"I am reasonably certain you didn't swoon the first time, madam," Blade said wryly at Felicity's side.

He was right, of course. Auntie Agatha had not truly swooned. Her aunt was merely being, *well*, Auntie Agatha. Melodramatic, grumpy, and rude, not always in that order. She had good intentions, but her execution was often lacking.

In this instance, Felicity could not blame her aunt for her shock.

Even Felicity could still scarcely believe she was marrying Blade Winter, the man she loved. The man who loved her too. The sight of him awaiting her in the library would forever be imprinted upon her memory—an inking of her own.

"You, sir, are a scoundrel," Auntie Agatha announced, opening her eyes to pin Blade with a disapproving glare. "My beloved niece cannot possibly marry you."

"Auntie Agatha," Felicity intervened, "I have already agreed to wed Mr. Winter."

"Your father has not given his approval of such a match," her aunt argued. "Nor would he."

"My father will be happy for me to wed Mr. Winter, particularly when he learns Mr. Winter is willing to provide Esme and Cassandra with dowries and help to ease his debts. Truly, I could not ask for a better husband."

Not because of those reasons, but Blade's generosity was undeniably sweet.

"He is a bastard," Auntie Agatha exclaimed, *sotto voce*.

Unfortunately, her whisper carried to Blade.

"The bastard son of a Covent Garden doxy, if you must know," he said, shrugging. "Fortunately, Lady Felicity is willing to overlook my sins and give me a chance to redeem myself."

I love you, she mouthed at him.

He winked.

"Saw that, dear girl," Auntie Agatha said with a harrumph, banging the floor of the yellow salon—where they had chosen to privately deliver their news to her—with her cane. "You cannot possibly be in love with this rakehell. He has a terrible reputation."

Yes, he did.

But Felicity loved him anyway. He was more than the sum of his past. More than his parentage or where he lived or what he had done. He was the man who kissed her with such gentleness, it made her want to weep. The man who held her heart in his hands.

"He is a fine man, Auntie Agatha," she defended Blade. "I could not ask for a better husband."

Her aunt snorted. "You could certainly ask. What happened to Lord Chilton?"

"I do not love him," she said. "I love Mr. Winter."

"If Chilton would prefer his nose to remain unbroken, he

will never again sneak away to the mistletoe with my future wife," Blade clipped.

Auntie Agatha fanned herself. "You see, my dear? The man is a brute."

He was hardly a brute.

"A brute turned gentleman," Blade corrected, grinning, his dimple reappearing.

Was it her imagination, or was Auntie Agatha flushing beneath his rakish regard?

Her aunt fanned herself some more. "A gentleman, you say? Hmm."

"When you get to know Mr. Winter as I have, you will realize he is perfect for me in every way," Felicity told her aunt, and that much was the utter truth.

Her future husband's gaze connected with hers. His smile said more than words could, and it warmed her heart.

"I love your niece, and I promise to do everything I can to be a good husband and make her happy," Blade told her aunt.

Auntie Agatha flapped her fan with more determination than ever. "You had better, Mr. Winter. Or you will answer to me and my cane."

She thumped it on the floor to emphasize her point.

The door to the salon clicked open to reveal Lady Emilia, wearing her angelic smile. "Do forgive me for the interruption, but I was wondering if we might get started talking about modistes for Lady Cassandra's and Lady Esme's seasons."

"I am generally considered an arbiter of fashion," Auntie Agatha disclosed with the air of a queen.

Lady Emilia settled in with Felicity's aunt, and the two began a discussion about the merits of lace. Felicity had not realized Blade had drifted nearer to her until his lips hovered at her ear, making her shiver.

"Come away with me," Blade whispered, his hand finding hers, their fingers lacing together in a gesture that felt as natural as it did familiar.

"Where to?" she asked softly.

His bright-blue eyes were warm with sensual intent. "Anywhere I can kiss my future wife."

Oh, she liked the sound of that. Kissing him and the notion of her future as his wife both.

"You can kiss me everywhere," she murmured as they collectively began easing away from Auntie Agatha and Lady Emilia.

"Everywhere?" he teased with a smirk that made heat slide through her. "Do not tempt me with a good time."

Another few steps, and they had quietly extricated themselves from the yellow salon. Still holding hands, they made their way to the nearest chamber, which was blessedly empty. The door was scarcely even closed before Felicity threw herself into Blade's arms.

This was where she belonged, in the arms of the man she loved, his wicked lips on hers.

168

Epilogue

"$\mathcal{I}$ HAVE A gift for you. Two gifts, actually."

Blade's heart, which was already ridiculously full and large after having finally made Lady Felicity Hughes his earlier that morning before their families—Winters, Hughes, and even her curmudgeonly aunt—swelled larger. He was grateful, so bloody grateful, for Felicity's love.

He took his wife, who was wearing a thin night rail he could not wait to peel off her lovely body, into his arms. Her hair was unbound, sending chestnut curls down her back, all the better for him to bury his face in. He inhaled deeply of her floral, beloved scent, and relished the feeling of her softness pressed to his body.

"You are gift enough," he said tenderly, rubbing his cheek over the silken skeins of her tresses.

Her arms went around his waist, holding him tight. She pressed her face to his throat, kissing him there. "I am part of the gift."

His cockstand was instant. "I like the sound of that, love."

"Naughty man." Her throaty laugh only made him harder.

She kissed his pulse, which had begun to pound in anticipation. He had played the gentleman—mostly—whilst awaiting their nuptials. He had licked her until she spent in the carriage back to London after cleverly orchestrating Auntie

Agatha's mistaken placement in a carriage with Gen, Demon, and Gavin. His trick had only been successful until they had reached the coaching inn.

Auntie Dragon had not been amused.

Felicity had been sated.

Worth it.

"Let me show you just how naughty this man can be," he said. "I promise you will appreciate my efforts."

That was not an exaggeration. He had every intention of making her come until she could not move this evening. The day had been long, with the wedding, the celebration with their families, and then settling in at their new Mayfair home, which was quite near to Dom's and Devil's homes.

That had been a feat that required Blade selling his ownership in The Devil's Spawn and stepping down from his position there. Now, he was overseeing the waterworks for his family and beginning a partnership with Devereaux on a cutlery factory. Their marriage had not been as hasty as he would have preferred, but he had also known he needed to enter this union with her as a new man.

No more troublesome Blade Winter, fighting duels, carving up cheats and scoundrels at the Devil's Spawn with his blades. No more rakehell and scoundrel. From the moment he had realized he was in love with Felicity, all he had wanted was to be her man.

The man she deserved.

He was not quite that man yet, but he would continue working at it, and he would continue loving her.

"I know I will appreciate your efforts, my love." She kissed her way up his throat to his ear. The minx's tongue ran over the shell. "It has been far too long since we have been alone. Lying in bed, touching myself while I thought of you, was dismal comfort."

"Hell," he groaned, thrusting into her so she could feel the length of his throbbing erection through the thin barriers of his banyan and her night rail. "You touched yourself, love?"

The mere thought was enough to make a bead of mettle seep from his tip, and he had not kissed her yet.

"I did." She kissed across his jaw now.

By God, she was seducing him. So much for being the seasoned rakehell. All it took was one woman to bring him to his knees. The right woman. This one.

"Where?" he rasped, though he knew he should not.

It was so wicked, the notion of her lying alone at night, touching herself until she spent as he had done.

"My pearl," she said, using the word he had taught her for that special, plump bud.

She kissed her way to his lips, her tongue flicking over the seam.

"Did you spend?" he asked on a growl of pure need.

"Yes," she whispered, and then she kissed him.

The union of their mouths was deep and dark and carnal, filled with promise and love. He was thankful every day that her kitten had chosen his bed to get lost beneath and that his half siblings had done their damnedest to matchmake and throw them together. She was everything he wanted, everything he had needed without realizing it.

Their tongues tangled. The thought of Miss Wilhelmina had him lifting his head prematurely.

"What is the matter?" she asked, breathless.

She knew him so well.

"How is Miss Wilhelmina getting on with Mr. Spoony?" he asked.

He did not think it was a mistake that a little orange cat—scruffy and starved—had found its way to him in the rookery whilst he had been awaiting the Mayfair House's purchase to be completed. He had taken the bugger in, feeding him, cleaning him. And the furred scamp had rather made his imprint upon Blade's heart.

"I still cannot believe you named him Mr. Spoony."

"It was either that or Arsehole," he defended. "The first three nights I had him, he kept me up all night with his caterwauling, and then he attacked my window dressings with his claws."

Felicity smiled up at him. "You have a good heart, Blade Winter. Just as I've always known. Our mister and miss were getting on quite well when I checked on them earlier, but I am not certain Miss Wilhelmina will ever like him well enough to share her liver. But never mind that. Let me show you your gifts before you distract me."

Hell. Although he had already given her his gift—a room just for her to sketch in, decorated with all her favorite colors—he still felt guilty for not having something else.

"Fair enough," he grumbled.

She extricated herself from his arms and crossed the chamber, retrieving something she kept behind her back, before handing it over with a shy smile. "Here you are. I do hope you like it. As I said, I am not talented, but I enjoy the art."

He stared down at the sketched likeness in his hands. It was him, holding the kitten-sized Miss Wilhelmina by the scruff of her neck in his chamber at Abingdon Hall. Her talent was astounding. And undeniable. He had not pressed her to share it with him, sensing her shyness. Now, he could not fathom why.

"My God, love, this is incredible."

"It is you," she said, her cheeks going pink.

"Aye, I'd recognize my sorry gob anywhere. But that is not what is incredible. 'Tis your talent. I am…astounded." He paused, searching for finer words and finding none. "Thank you for this beautiful gift. I love it, and I love you."

She beamed, rising on her toes to press a chaste kiss to his lips. "I am so pleased you like it, darling."

"Like does not begin to describe the way I feel." Humbled, he took the sketch to a nearby table and placed it there. "It is incredible, just as you are."

"Good. Now here is the other part of your gift." She stepped back and lifted the hem of her night rail, putting her right ankle forward.

For a moment, he could do nothing but admire the elegant point of her toes and the curve of her calf, without the hindrance of stockings. All that creamy skin. *Christ.* Her ankles.

But then he spied it—an inking just above the protrusion of her anklebone. A dagger.

"My God, Felicity." He dropped to his knees, taking her foot in his hand, examining the beautiful work. "Did Gen do this?"

"Yes." Felicity nodded, her expression hesitant. Almost shy. "Do you like it? I wanted something to show I am yours, now and forever. It seemed…right."

He was speechless. The ink was healed. She must have asked Gen to give her the mark shortly after their return to London.

"You do not dislike it, do you?" Her tone was nervous. "Pray do not be angry with your sister. She was hesitant to do it, but I insisted."

He rubbed his thumb over the blade, the hilt. Such intricate detail. So beautiful. And she had done this for him. The inkings were painful, an arduous process. His brave, beautiful lady. He could not love her more.

"Dislike it?" He pressed a reverent kiss to her there. "I

bloody well love it."

Her smile returned. "I wanted to make you happy."

"Always. You always make me happy."

"Oh, Blade." There were tears glistening in her eyes, and that was not what he wanted now.

What he wanted was her utter, absolute pleasure.

"Since I am already where I belong, on my knees for you," he said, giving her his best rakish grin, "take off your night rail, love."

Her lips parted, her hazel eyes darkening. "If you insist."

She grasped her demure gown in both hands and lifted it over her head, tossing it behind her. His beautiful wife was naked before him. *Fuck*, he was the luckiest chap in England, and he knew it.

"I insist," he said as he cupped her arse and pulled her forward.

He sucked her pearl and sank a finger deep inside her slick channel simultaneously. Crooking his finger, he found the place he knew she was most sensitive. It had been too long since he had last pleasured her, and she did not last. She came gloriously, crying out, her fingernails digging into his shoulders through the silk of his banyan.

He rose to his full height and claimed her lips, letting her taste herself on his tongue as he kissed her. They fell into the bed together, and he worked his way to her beautiful breasts, sucking, licking, and nipping, while he played with her cunny. Slipping a finger deep, then another, working and stretching her. Toying with her pearl until she spent again.

At last, he guided his cock to her entrance. "I love you, Felicity Winter."

"Oh," she said on a moan, body arching from the bed as he entered her in one swift thrust. "I love you too. So much."

They came together, her sheath tightening on him, the

white-hot desire taking him by surprise. Heat licked up his spine, and he exploded, burying himself to the hilt and filling her with his seed.

Breathless, boneless, and mindless once again, he collapsed against her, reveling in the tandem pounding of their hearts, the closeness of their bodies, the intimacy of skin on skin. Her arms went around him, holding him tight.

He had found the place where he belonged. With this woman.

Nothing had ever felt so real, and nothing had ever felt so right.

She was his, and he was hers.

Forever.

THE END

Dear Reader,

Thank you for reading *Winter's Whispers*! I hope you loved this tenth book in my *The Wicked Winters* series and that Blade and Felicity touched your heart and made you laugh along the way. We all need more laughter, don't we? And love. We need that, too. I also hope you enjoyed the glimpses of previous couples in the series. If this is the first book you've picked up in the series, you can catch the happily ever afters of all the other couples mentioned in *Winter's Whispers* in books 1-6. As always, thank you for spending your precious time reading my books!

Please consider leaving an honest review of *Winter's Woman*. Reviews are greatly appreciated! If you'd like to keep up to date with my latest releases and series news, sign up for my newsletter here or follow me on Amazon or BookBub. Join my reader's group on Facebook for bonus content, early excerpts, giveaways, and more.

There are more Winters on the way. If you'd like a preview of *Winter's Waltz*, Book Eleven in *The Wicked Winters* series, featuring fierce, eccentric, breeches-wearing Gen Winter and the ne'er-do-well lord she's about to reform, do read on.

Until next time,

Scarlett

Winter's Waltz

The Wicked Winters Book Eleven

BY

SCARLETT SCOTT

The Marquess of Sundenbury needs to stay out of trouble. Genevieve Winter needs a favor. What could go wrong? Only everything…

Sundenbury has a gambling problem. Genevieve has a Sundenbury problem. Namely, she has been tasked with keeping an eye on the scandalous lord. Gen has plans to open a ladies' gaming establishment, and while she's saddled with London's biggest ne'er do well, he has to make himself useful. In exchange for her aid, the marquess must help her gain the ladylike polish she requires to lure in her lucrative clientele.

Max, Marquess of Sundenbury, is the undisputed black sheep of his family. With his gambling debts mounting and a ducal father who has cut off the purse strings, he needs to reform his reputation and find a wealthy bride. His plan? Take a month away from society, give the wagging tongues time to settle down, then reemerge a changed man, and all that folderol.

But he never bargained for the hellion in breeches who amazes him with her sharp wit, sharper tongue, and undeniable beauty. Gen wants nothing to do with a handsome scoundrel like Max, no matter how sinful his kisses or tempting his embrace. An independent lady gaming hell owner and a penniless lord who can't stay away from the hazard table could not be more wrong for each other.

Or mayhap, just mayhap, they could not be more right.

Chapter One

East London, 1815

THE MARQUESS OF Sundenbury was not going to last more than ten minutes in the East End. Genevieve Winter was never more certain of it than when she found him seated in *her* chair at *her* desk, his polished boots propped upon *her* ledgers, grinning like the stupid, handsome fiend he was.

He was not going to last because she was going to murder him.

Poison, she decided. He was too pretty to suffer the agony of gunshot or the blade. Mayhap she could slip hemlock into his tea.

"Miss Winter," he said, not bothering to rise.

The omission suited her perfectly fine, she told herself. Gen did not prefer to be treated as a lady. She wore breeches, shirt, cravat, and boots this morning. It was ever so much more comfortable than stays and gowns. Why did chaps get to claim the best garments for themselves?

"What the hell are you doing in my office, you spoony twat?" she demanded.

He winced, as if her vulgar words caused him physical pain. Gen hoped they did.

"Is that any way to greet the man who will be your companion—indeed, your saving grace—for the next month?"

"Saving grace?" She snorted, crossing her arms over her chest and pinning him with a glare. "Pain in my arse, more like."

What the devil had she been thinking when she had agreed to this bloody addlepated idea of her half brothers' wives? Lady Addy and Lady Evie, twins who were married to her half brothers Dom and Devil, had suggested the plan to her after their brother's last embarrassment.

Having been banished from The Devil's Spawn thanks to his inability to control his gambling, he had wormed his way into the rival gaming hell owned by the Suttons. And he had promptly gotten tap-hackled and lost ten thousand pounds.

He had also had his purse strings cut by his father the duke.

Fitting, in her opinion. The old duke ought to have boxed his ears and sent him to Elba with Boney while he was at it.

Sundenbury quirked a brow at her, and then the blighter lifted a cigar to his lips, giving it a puff and sending a cloud of smoke in her direction. "You have a fine arse, Miss Winter. I would hate to cause it any pain."

He sounded so polite, with those crisp, aristocratic accents of his. And yet he looked thoroughly dissolute. His cravat was undone, and he was down to his shirtsleeves. His wavy, dark hair was ruffled, as if some obliging wench had recently run her fingers through it.

She probably had. Gen would make her next order of business a trip to the ladies employed by The Devil's Spawn. Her unwanted charge was not to be cozying up with ladybirds. He was supposed to be staying out of trouble. No gambling. No whoring. No drinking.

No to any of the things an empty-headed, gorgeous-faced lord like Sundenbury ordinarily did. And why did he have to be so handsome, anyway, curse him? Gen governed herself with stern rules. When she had been younger and stupider, she had found herself at the mercy of a handsome scoundrel. Never again.

Good thing men like the marquess had no effect upon her.

She stalked forward and plucked the cigar from Sundenbury's long, elegant fingers. "No smoking in my office. It bloody well stinks, and I'll not have it. And if you dare to say another word about my arse, I'll break your fingers."

"No need for such anger, pet." He gave her the sort of grin she was sure made every other lady melt.

Not Gen. She tossed his cigar into the fire, then turned back to the intruder still seated at her desk. "Do not call me *pet*."

"Or what? You shall break my fingers?" he asked, grin deepening.

For some reason, she found herself staring at his lips. They were wide and full. The sort of lips a man should not possess. The sudden warmth blossoming inside her was as traitorous as it was unwanted. Ruthlessly, she quashed it.

"No," she told him calmly. "If you call me *pet* again, I will break your nose. Don't suppose you'd have all the ladies begging to drop to their knees if you had a crooked beak."

"When the ladies are on their knees for me, they aren't looking at my nose, Miss Winter."

For some reason, the insinuation in his words made her cheeks go hot. Which was impossible. She had been surrounded by men from the time she had been a tiny girl. First her brother Gavin, then her half brothers Demon, Blade, Dom, and Devil. Nothing could embarrass her.

Irritation sliced through her. This silly lordling would not best her at her own game.

"Hmm," she said. "They are probably looking for your

prick, unable to find it on account of it being so *small*."

"There is nothing about my cock that is small, pet," he purred.

"I warned you about your nose, Sundenbury."

She stalked toward him, her boots pounding on the carpets. By the time she rounded her desk, he had risen at last, and he was still smiling, curse him. Her body's reaction to him was infuriating. Instinct, she told herself. He was a handsome man. She was a woman. That was all. There was nothing a disreputable ne'er-do-well who could not handle himself at the green baize had to offer her.

But he was also surprisingly stealthy for a lord she had supposed to be cupshot when she had entered the room. He caught her elbows and spun her with ease, then used his larger, taller, more powerful body to force her backward. There was nowhere to go save her desk.

Her bottom landed on her much-abused ledgers.

He insinuated himself between her parted thighs and flattened his palms on the desk, trapping her. "Go on then, Miss Winter. Give me your worst. I dare you."

Want more? Get *Winter's Waltz!*

Don't miss Scarlett's other romances!

(Listed by Series)

Complete Book List
scarlettscottauthor.com/books

HISTORICAL ROMANCE

Heart's Temptation
A Mad Passion (Book One)
Rebel Love (Book Two)
Reckless Need (Book Three)
Sweet Scandal (Book Four)
Restless Rake (Book Five)
Darling Duke (Book Six)
The Night Before Scandal (Book Seven)

Wicked Husbands
Her Errant Earl (Book One)
Her Lovestruck Lord (Book Two)
Her Reformed Rake (Book Three)
Her Deceptive Duke (Book Four)
Her Missing Marquess (Book Five)
Her Virtuous Viscount (Book Six)

League of Dukes
Nobody's Duke (Book One)
Heartless Duke (Book Two)
Dangerous Duke (Book Three)
Shameless Duke (Book Four)
Scandalous Duke (Book Five)
Fearless Duke (Book Six)

Notorious Ladies of London
Lady Ruthless (Book One)
Lady Wallflower (Book Two)
Lady Reckless (Book Three)
Lady Wicked (Book Four)

The Wicked Winters
Wicked in Winter (Book One)
Wedded in Winter (Book Two)
Wanton in Winter (Book Three)
Wishes in Winter (Book 3.5)
Willful in Winter (Book Four)
Wagered in Winter (Book Five)
Wild in Winter (Book Six)
Wooed in Winter (Book Seven)
Winter's Wallflower (Book Eight)
Winter's Woman (Book Nine)
Winter's Whispers (Book Ten)
Winter's Waltz (Book Eleven)
Winter's Widow (Book Twelve)
Winter's Warrior (Book Thirteen)

Stand-alone Novella
Lord of Pirates

CONTEMPORARY ROMANCE

Love's Second Chance
Reprieve (Book One)
Perfect Persuasion (Book Two)
Win My Love (Book Three)

Coastal Heat
Loved Up (Book One)

About the Author

USA Today and Amazon bestselling author Scarlett Scott writes steamy Victorian and Regency romance with strong, intelligent heroines and sexy alpha heroes. She lives in Pennsylvania with her Canadian husband, adorable identical twins, and one TV-loving dog.

A self-professed literary junkie and nerd, she loves reading anything, but especially romance novels, poetry, and Middle English verse. Catch up with her on her website www.scarlettscottauthor.com. Hearing from readers never fails to make her day.

Scarlett's complete book list and information about upcoming releases can be found at www.scarlettscottauthor.com.

Connect with Scarlett! You can find her here:
Join Scarlett Scott's reader's group on Facebook for early excerpts, giveaways, and a whole lot of fun!
Sign up for her newsletter here.
scarlettscottauthor.com/contact
Follow Scarlett on Amazon
Follow Scarlett on BookBub
www.instagram.com/scarlettscottauthor
www.twitter.com/scarscoromance
www.pinterest.com/scarlettscott
www.facebook.com/AuthorScarlettScott

Printed in Great Britain
by Amazon